Hawai'i Island
LEGENDS

Pīkoi, Pele and Others

Hawai'i Island LEGENDS

Pīkoi, Pele and Others

compiled by
Mary Kawena Pūku'i

retold by
Caroline Curtis

illustrated by
Don Robinson

Kamehameha Schools Press
Honolulu
1996

Kamehameha Schools Bernice Pauahi Bishop Estate

Previously published as:
Pikoi and Other Legends of the Island of Hawaii
Copyright © 1949 (Reprinted 1971, 1983),
This edition copyright © 1996 by
Kamehameha Schools Bernice Pauahi Bishop Estate

09 08 07 06 05 04 03 02 01 00 99   5 4 3 2

Inquiries should be addressed to:
Kamehameha Schools Press
1887 Makuakāne Street
Honolulu, Hawaiʻi 96817

The paper used in this publication meets the minimum requirements of
American National Standard for Information Sciences—
Permanence of Paper for Printed Library Materials,
ANSI Z39.48-1984.

Printed in the United States of America

ISBN 0-87336-032-X

Hawai'i Island LEGENDS

Pīkoi, Pele and Others

Contents

Preface

When Polynesian people came to Hawai'i, hundreds of years ago, they brought legends. We know this because the same stories and similar hero names are found in other Polynesian groups. Other legends grew about historical events in our islands, about real people and places. Some are very old while others have grown in recent times.

As all these stories were told and retold changes crept in. While the main story was the same, details became very different. No one can say that one version of a story is right and the others wrong. At the end of each legend I have given the principal source used. I, too, have made changes.

Many of these stories are about chiefs, for they led a varied and colorful life and the common people liked to hear about them. In old Hawai'i each valley, from mountain to sea, was a district with its district chief. Sometimes one chief made himself ruler of several districts or of an entire island. Thus he became a high chief with lesser chiefs under him.

We tell and read legends not only for enjoyment but also because they help us understand people who lived long ago.

C.C.

Acknowledgments

We express sincere appreciation to the members of the staff of Kamehameha Schools and to other teachers and librarians whose suggestions and criticism have helped in the making of this book.

M.K.P. and C.C.

Pīkoi

Pīkoi

Rat Shooting

"**W**hy is that crowd down the valley? Brother! What are all those people doing?"

Pīkoi's brother was preparing food for the *imu* and did not hear the boy's question. Pīkoi and his father had come from Kaua'i the day before. They had come to Mānoa Valley on O'ahu to visit a married sister. A crowd the very first day! Pīkoi must find out what was going on.

At first he went slowly down the trail, watching the people eagerly. He saw someone with a bow and arrows. Rat shooting! That was a sport the boy loved and in a moment he was running.

Pīkoi reached the crowd and pushed his way among them. He bumped a tall woman who turned to him angrily. "What are you doing here?" she asked. "Why do you push in beside your chiefess?"

Pīkoi did not quite understand that this woman was the chiefess—the high chiefess of O'ahu. "It is rat shooting, isn't it?" he asked eagerly. "I love rat shooting."

The chiefess must have liked the boy's love of her favorite sport, for she spoke good-naturedly now. "Can you shoot rats?"

"A little."

"That man with a red *lei* and with a bow in his hand is Ma'inele," the chiefess said. "He is the best rat shooter on O'ahu. I am looking for a champion to shoot against him. Do you want to be my champion?"

The chiefess was joking. A boy could not shoot against Ma'inele! But Pīkoi did not know she was joking. "Oh yes," he said. "May I use your arrows?"

The chiefess let him take her arrows and Pīkoi looked at them carefully. "These are not good," he said slowly. He could not shoot against the champion with poor arrows. Just then, out of the corner of his eye, the boy saw his father. He had followed Pīkoi with a bundle in his hand. "My bow and arrows!" the boy thought. He broke the poor arrows of the chiefess and let the pieces fall to the ground.

She was angry this time. "You bad, bad boy!" she exclaimed. "You have broken all my arrows! Now I can't get a champion to shoot against Ma'inele!"

"I will shoot for you," said Pīkoi. "I told you I would." People had heard the angry voice of the chiefess and they came crowding around.

"So you are going to shoot against me?" a new voice asked.

Pīkoi looked up into the face of Ma'inele. "Yes," he said. "What is the game?"

"Fifteen rats. The one who first kills fifteen rats is the winner," Ma'inele answered. "Will you shoot first or shall I?"

"You shoot first," the boy answered, and everybody shouted with laughter.

"He's a clever boy!" they said. "He tells Ma'inele to shoot first. Ma'inele is sure to get his fifteen rats. Then the boy won't have to shoot at all. He is beaten without ever showing that he can't shoot! Oh, he's a clever one!"

But Pīkoi did not hear the laughter and jokes. "You shoot, Ma'inele," he said again. "Look! There's a rat!" He said this in an excited whisper. "There by that weed stalk! Do you see?"

"I have eyes!" Ma'inele answered as he made ready an arrow.

"Good! You got it!" Pīkoi exclaimed. "There is another one, a big one beside the *kamani* tree. Quick, Ma'inele.

"Good! Two rats! There is one way over there—"

"Keep still!" warned Ma'inele. "I shot rats before you were born. I can see them without your help!"

And he shot again and again—twelve—thirteen—fourteen! The people watching smiled at each other. "There won't be any left for the boy to shoot," they said.

Ma'inele stood looking around. Everyone looked. Ma'inele must have killed every rat in that part of the valley! Surely there was not one to be seen.

"There's one!" exclaimed Pīkoi in an excited whisper. "In the weeds!" He was pointing.

Ma'inele looked carefully. "I don't see it," he said.

"No, you can't see the rat—only the whiskers. It is eating weed seeds and you can see its whiskers move. Shoot the whiskers, Ma'inele!"

Ma'inele turned angrily toward the boy. "Whiskers!" he said. "I am a champion rat shooter! I have good sight! I have shot rats in the head. I have shot rats in the front legs. I have shot rats in the hind legs. But I never shot one in the whiskers. There is no rat there. Let us see you shoot a rat where there is no rat!"

Pīkoi kept his eyes fixed on the clump of weeds, watching the whiskers move as the rat ate. He knew his father was standing close behind him and he held out his hand.

His father put bow and arrow into the outstretched hand. Pīkoi chanted a prayer. While he prayed he raised the bow and took aim. He did not once take his eyes from those moving whiskers. His arrow whistled and Pīkoi drew a long breath. "I got the rat!" he said.

The chiefess nodded to a servant who ran in among the weeds and held up Pīkoi's arrow for all to see. There were three rats on the arrow and one had been shot through the whiskers! People looked at each other in great surprise. There was no laughter now.

Pīkoi held out his hand for another arrow. "Not that one," he whispered to his father. "That is not a good ratting arrow. I need a long one—a strong one."

At last he had an arrow that pleased him. He bent his bow. Then he stood looking off among the trees and prayed for power to shoot well. His prayer ended in a whisper: "Hush! Be still. There are the rats!"

His arrow flew. Everyone was watching, but the arrow went among the bushes and no one could see what it hit. There was a squeak. Then all was still.

A servant ran to get the arrow. The crowd saw him stoop down among the bushes. Then he called to another man to help him. A moment later they held up Pīkoi's arrow, loaded with rats!

The people had been very quiet, almost holding their breath. Now they began to shout.

"Fifteen! Why the boy got more than fifteen with one shot!"

"Wonderful!"

"This is something to tell our grandchildren!"

"Maʻinele has been beaten by a boy."

Pīkoi got his arrows and he and his father went quietly home to the feast the brother had made ready.

Enemies of the Chief

Keawenui, high chief of Hawaiʻi, stood looking up the barren mountain slope toward the forest. Nothing! No one running down the trail. And yet many days had passed.

"O Heavenly One, may you live long."

Keawenui had not heard the man who now knelt before him. "Speak," he said.

"O Heavenly One, many days have passed since your canoe makers went into the forest. Is it not time to haul the new canoe down to Hilo?"

"It is time," the chief answered, "but no word has come. The men have not sent a runner to say that the canoe is ready." He turned again to search the mountain trail with his keen eyes.

"I see someone!" he exclaimed. The tiny figure seemed to move slowly. It was lost to sight then seen again, nearer and larger.

For a long time the chief and man watched. "It must be the runner," said the man as the figure became more plain.

But the chief's eyes were very keen. "No," he said, "it is my *kahuna,* himself. What is wrong that the old man comes to bring the news?"

The figure drew near. It was the figure of a white-haired man, yet it came on at a strong, steady pace. At last the old *kahuna* knelt before Keawenui and greeted him. "May you live long, O Heavenly One!"

"What news do you bring, O Kahuna?" Keawenui asked.

"The canoe is not yet hollowed," the old man answered. "The chief has enemies in the forest."

"Enemies!" exclaimed Keawenui in a terrible voice. "Am I not high chief of this island of Hawai'i? What men dare to raise their hands against me?"

"No men, O Heavenly One. Birds!"

"Speak, Kahuna. I do not understand your riddle."

"I chose a tree. It was a *koa,* tall and straight, fit for a chief's canoe. We cut it down, trimmed away the branches and shaped the canoe. All had gone well and our hearts were glad.

"We started to hollow the canoe. Suddenly we heard voices from above us. 'Bad luck! Bad luck!' they called.

'That canoe will have bad luck! The log is rotten. When it is in the ocean it will turn bottom up.'

"High above us in a treetop sat two birds. They called again their bad-luck cry, then flew away to the deep blue of heaven. We turned to our work, but the words of those birds were true words. There were rotten spots in that *koa* log."

"Why did you not choose another tree?"

"O Heavenly One, I did. Another and another. Three great trees we have cut down, trimmed and shaped. Only when all that work was done did the birds cry their bad-luck cry. Only then did we find rotten places. These birds are your enemies! They will not let the chief have a new canoe."

"My enemies shall die!" the chief exclaimed. He turned to the man who knelt nearby. "Run to the rat shooters of Hilo," he commanded. "Tell them it is my will that they go up into the forest with my *kahuna* and kill these birds. None shall cry, 'Bad luck!' to Keawenui and live!"

The command of the chief was obeyed. Some days later the rat shooters returned to Hilo hanging their heads in shame. "O Heavenly One, we could not kill those birds," they said. "They perched high on a tree. We bent our heads back until our necks ached. We gazed at those small birds and aimed our arrows. Again and again we shot, but no arrow could hit them."

"Birds!" the chief cried. "Shall two little birds bring bad luck to Keawenui and not be punished? Surely there is someone on this island who knows how to use bow and arrows."

He called for runners and sent them around the island. "Call the best rat shooters on Hawai'i," he commanded. "Tell them to come to the forest up there on the mountainside. Tell them the high chief, himself, will

watch their shooting. He will give a reward to the one who rids him of these enemies. Go!"

Some days later the chief, with his men, went to the forest. They found the canoe makers ready. Another large *koa* tree had been cut, trimmed and shaped. There lay the chief's canoe on the ground. But it was still solid, for the inside had not been cut away. Several rat shooters had come and all waited for their chief.

"Where are these enemies you talk of?" Keawenui asked. He looked long into the treetops. "I see no birds."

One of the canoe makers lifted his stone adze and struck the canoe, beginning to hollow it. The chief saw two small birds fly from the blue sky and perch high in a tall tree. Then he heard their hoarse cry: "Bad luck! Bad luck! That canoe will have bad luck! The log is rotten. When it is in the ocean it will turn bottom up."

The chief turned to the rat shooter nearest him. "You first," he said. "A reward from your chief if you kill his enemies!" He watched the man bend back and take careful aim. He watched the arrow fly. It fell short.

"A weak shot!" Keawenui said and motioned to the next rat shooter. This man bent his bow far back and let his arrow fly. It went straight toward the birds, but they moved a little. The arrow went between them.

As man after man shot and missed, the chief grew angry. Then he became afraid. Could no one kill these strange enemies? Would he never have a new canoe?

He lifted his head with sudden hope. "Ma'inele!" he said. "I have heard that Ma'inele is the champion rat shooter of O'ahu. Let us send for him."

He turned to a trusted man. "You shall go," he said. "Take my own double canoe. Take strong paddlers. Go to Waikīkī on O'ahu and give this message to the high chief: 'Keawenui needs help. He needs the help of Ma'inele, that great rat shooter. Let Ma'inele come to Hawai'i and rid the chief of his enemies. Let him do this and

Keawenui will give him the young chiefess for his wife.'"
Keawenui did not know that there was a better rat shooter
than Ma'inele!

ॐ ॐ ॐ

Years had passed since Pīkoi had won the rat shooting contest in Mānoa. Now he was a man and living at
Waikīkī as one of the high chief's men. He was a strong,
skillful, clever young man and a fine companion. He had
many friends, and one enemy. Ma'inele had never forgotten that he had been beaten by a boy.

One day Pīkoi saw strangers coming from the landing place. Men from another island? He watched them go
toward the home of the high chief. Then he went to look
at their canoe. A double canoe! And was that not a red
sail rolled up in the bottom? It must be the canoe of a
chief. Why had it come, Pīkoi wondered, and where was
it going? If only he could go in it! Pīkoi longed to see
other islands.

After a time the young man saw the strangers return
to the beach. Ma'inele was with them. Ma'inele! "Where
are you going?" Pīkoi asked.

Ma'inele walked on as if he had not heard.

Pīkoi followed eagerly. "Where are you going?" he
asked the paddlers. "To Maui? To Hawai'i? Oh, take me
with you! I want to see those islands."

The men pushed off the canoe and stepped in, but
no one answered Pīkoi.

"Take me with you," he begged again. "I am a strong
paddler."

The canoe was gone. Pīkoi watched it cross the reef
and reach the great waves beyond. Why should Ma'inele
go and he be left behind?

"Perhaps you can go in the small canoe." Pīkoi turned quickly to a man who stood near, also watching.

"The small canoe?" he asked, not understanding.

"Yes. A small canoe came from Hilo with the large one. A man named Waiākea was paddling. I think he went off to visit friends. Perhaps he will come back to Waikīkī."

"I shall watch for Waiākea," said Pīkoi.

For a long time the young man waited at the landing place. At last he saw a small canoe flying along before the quick strokes of one paddler. As it came near the landing the man shouted, "Has the double canoe gone? The canoe of Keawenui?"

"To Hilo?" asked Pīkoi. "Yes. But take me with you. I am a good paddler. You and I together can paddle fast and reach Hilo before the large canoe."

"Good!" Waiākea answered. "Get your things. I have to get fresh water."

While Waiākea filled his water gourds Pīkoi got food. He also got his bundle wrapped in *kapa*—his bow and arrows. Soon the canoe was flying through the waves. Waiākea was glad of the help of this young man of Oʻahu. He did not know his name and he did not care. Both men paddled fast and wasted no time in talk.

They came in sight of Molokaʻi. Suddenly Waiākea heard his companion exclaim, "There's a big rat!"

Waiākea thought the rat was in the canoe and turned to look. The stranger from Oʻahu had bow and arrow in his hands and was getting ready to shoot. "Keep paddling!" he said. "Keep the canoe steady."

Waiākea turned to his paddling but he was filled with wonder. Shoot what? Where? What was that young man talking about?

"I got it!" Pīkoi said. He began to paddle and the canoe, again, flew through the waves.

"What are you talking about?" asked Waiākea without turning.

"The big rat I shot. It is trying to get free of my arrow. We must paddle fast and get to it."

"Where?"

"On Moloka‘i. It is quiet now. It must be dead. But let us paddle to the shore for I want to get my arrow."

Waiākea watched his companion wade ashore. He watched him pull his arrow from a large rat. Then Pīkoi came running back, stepped into the canoe and took up his paddle. Waiākea stared. Who was this young man who could shoot a rat while far, far at sea? Wonderful!

The canoe came near Maui. "There's a rat—another big one!" Waiākea heard his companion say and turned to watch him shoot. The arrow flew swiftly until Waiākea could no longer see it. But Pīkoi was still watching. "Good!" he said. "I got that one!"

"Where?" Waiākea asked wonderingly as they paddled on.

"On the rocks there above Lāhainā. Don't you see the rat?"

No. Waiākea could hardly see Lāhainā! Could a man really shoot so far and kill a rat?

They reached Lāhainā and Waiākea saw his companion jump from the canoe, climb the rocks and pull an arrow from a large rat. He could hardly believe his own eyes!

The two paddled long. At last they came near Hawai‘i. "There's another big one!" said Pīkoi suddenly. "Upon the Kohala plain. Hold the canoe steady."

Waiākea watched his companion shoot. His eyes followed the arrow and saw it strike. He watched Pīkoi pull his arrow from a great rat. I don't know your name, he thought to himself, but I know you are a great rat shooter. I don't believe Ma‘inele can shoot rats better than you.

The two paddled on, but slowly now. They had breath for talk. Waiākea told Pīkoi about the enemies of Keawenui and why the canoes had gone to Waikīkī. "I don't believe Maʻinele is a better rat shooter than you are," he finished.

Pīkoi said nothing.

When they reached Hilo Waiākea took the young man to his home. "You stay with me," he said. "When it is time for the bird shooting, we can go up to the forest together."

So Pīkoi stayed with Waiākea. But before time for the bird shooting Pīkoi had made another friend. That was the young chiefess, the beautiful daughter of Keawenui. Pīkoi surfed with the young chiefess and her companion. They talked and sang together.

"Tonight there is to be a big feast for Maʻinele," Waiākea said one day. "Be ready early."

"I cannot go to the feast," Pīkoi answered. "I am going surfing."

"Surfing, you can surf any evening! You won't often taste a feast like this. Keawenui is giving it. You should see the food ready for the *imu!* Everyone is coming."

"I am not," Pīkoi said firmly. "I am going surfing."

And he spent the evening with the young chiefess and her companion. Pīkoi did not want Maʻinele to know that he had come to Hawaiʻi.

Waiākea slept late next morning and when he did awake was in a great hurry. "This is the day!" he told Pīkoi. "Come. We are going up to the forest to see Maʻinele shoot those bad-luck birds."

"Suppose Maʻinele shoots them," said Pīkoi, "what will be his reward?"

"The young chiefess," Waiākea answered. "If Maʻinele kills the chief's enemies Keawenui will make him his son-in-law."

So she is to be the reward, Pīkoi said to himself. Ma'inele is to marry that beautiful young woman! He must not. I can shoot better than Ma'inele. But what if Ma'inele kills the birds with his first arrow? Then he will get the young chiefess. Pīkoi did not like the thought.

"Come," said Waiākea. "Everyone is going up the mountain. We must hurry."

"I am going surfing," Pīkoi answered.

"And miss the bird shooting?" exclaimed Waiākea. "Why did you come to Hawai'i?"

"I shall come up later."

Pīkoi surfed with the young chiefess and her companion. His fears left him. He almost forgot about Ma'inele.

"Are you going to the bird shooting?" the chiefess asked as the three came out of the water.

"Are you?"

"No, but we will walk up the trail with you. You ought to go." So the three walked up the trail. It was hot and dusty until they reached the forest's edge. There they sat down. Pīkoi climbed *lehua* trees for red and white flowers and the young women made *lei*. A little breeze brought them the perfume of fern and *maile*. The air was full of bird songs. The three were quiet and very happy.

Suddenly they heard the sound of running on the trail above. With that sound all Pīkoi's fears returned. The bird shooting is over! he thought. Ma'inele has killed those enemies of the chief and he will marry this lovely young woman!

The next moment Waiākea came around a turn in the trial and stood before them. "Here you are!" he said to Pīkoi. "You must come with me at once. Keawenui is asking for you."

"The high chief has never seen me." Pīkoi answered. "He has never heard of me."

"He has now," said Waiākea. "Ma'inele could not shoot those birds. He is no better than the rat shooters of this island. He even called for a ladder so he could get close to these enemies of our chief. But he couldn't hit them. They are hard to shoot. But you can hit them. I know you can. I told Keawenui that I have a friend staying with me, an O'ahu man. I told him you are the best rat shooter in the world. 'Bring him here,' the chief commanded. 'Bring him at once.' You must come with me."

Pīkoi's heart was beating fast with joy when he heard that Ma'inele had not shot the birds. He was sure that he could. "I will come," he said.

Waiākea took Pīkoi to Keawenui. "O Heavenly One," he said, "this is the man from O'ahu."

Keawenui looked at Pīkoi sadly. Pīkoi could see that he had lost hope. He had said to himself, My enemies are stronger than I. One more rat shooter! He will be no better than the rest. Aloud he said, pointing, "There are my enemies, O Man of O'ahu. Shoot them if you can."

Pīkoi looked up at the treetops. His keen eyes saw the birds but he understood why others had failed. To shoot, a man must bend back until his neck ached. Even then the birds were tiny dots against the sky. He turned to Waiākea. "I need a large wooden bowl of water," he said.

A crowd had come to the forest to watch Ma'inele kill the birds. When he had failed they were very sad. Bad luck seemed to hang over their chief—over their island. Now a stranger had come. Did he think he could hit the birds? The best rat shooters of Hawai'i had failed. The great Ma'inele had failed. Who was this stranger, anyway? They crowded around to look at him.

Waiākea brought a large wooden bowl of water and set it on the ground. Pīkoi looked into the bowl, moved it and looked again. Then he stood gazing into it. The crowd began to laugh. A man came to shoot birds in the treetops, and then stood looking into a bowl of water on the ground! Laughter spread through the crowd.

But Pīkoi was not gazing idly. In the water he could see the reflection of the birds. He could watch them without bending backward or straining his eyes. He could watch them without those wise and evil birds knowing that he watched. Pīkoi did not hear the laughter of the crowd. He was watching the way the birds stretched their necks and moved their heads. He watched until he was sure of the best moment for a shot.

Then he prayed. He prayed as he had never prayed before, for so much was at stake. He must kill these birds with his first shot! He must win the young chiefess. As he chanted his prayer Pīkoi was gazing into the water mirror and watching for the right moment. Still looking down, he raised his bow above his head and aimed. For a moment he held the arrow.

> "I am Pīkoi,
> Pīkoi of Kaua'i.
> Hush! Be still!
> There are the birds up there.
> Here I am below.
> Fly, arrow of mine
> To the necks of the birds."

While Pīkoi chanted the crowd had grown quiet. With upturned faces they watched his arrow fly. They saw it pin the necks of those bad-luck birds together. The birds fell at their feet—dead. A great shout went up, a shout of wonder, joy and thankfulness. The enemies of the high chief were dead!

Pīkoi had won the young chiefess as his wife.

Pīkoi Sees Hawai'i

For many weeks Pīkoi and the young chiefess lived happily in Hilo. Pīkoi was son-in-law of the high chief now, a very great man. He enjoyed games and dances. More than all he enjoyed his wife.

But one day he said to her, "I came to see Hawai'i and I have seen only Hilo. I long to see all of this great island."

The young chiefess smiled at him. "Men long to see the world," she said. "Go then, my husband. Go to Puna first. It may be my father will go soon to our home in Waipi'o and we shall meet you there. Oh travel fast, Pīkoi, for I shall be very lonely."

Keawenui chose young men to go with Pīkoi, young men who knew the trails, young men who could travel steadily for days. These young men found Pīkoi a fine companion, a good walker and wonderful shooter of rats. By the time they reached Puna they were telling of the shots they had seen.

The chief of Puna gave a feast for the son-in-law of Keawenui. At the feast he heard stories of Pīkoi's shooting. "He shot rats we could not even see!" the young men said. "He killed the enemies of our high chief."

Hope woke in the heart of the Puna chief. "I, too, have enemies," he said to Pīkoi. "Two birds come at night to my gardens and the gardens of my people. They are eating all our food—*kalo,* sweet potatoes—everything. In the morning we find only empty vines. They are bringing us starvation."

"Has no one tried to kill them?" Pīkoi asked.

"No one can see them. They come only after dark. In the morning they are gone. But you, O Pīkoi! Your young men say that your sight is better than the sight of others. Your skill is greater than the skill of others. O Pīkoi, kill those enemies of mine."

"I will try," Pīkoi promised.

A little later he left the eating house. Darkness had come. Pīkoi stood looking over the chief's garden, bow and arrows in his hands. For a time his keen eyes searched the patches of *kalo* and potatoes. There! In among the sweet potato vines something moved! He saw those evil birds and shot. Looking around, Pīkoi saw that the men were still inside the eating house. He went to the potato patch to get his arrow but left the dead birds on the ground. Then he went back into the eating house to join the talk and laughter.

It was late when the men made ready for sleep. The chief led Pīkoi to the best pile of mats. "This is your place, my friend," he said. "May you sleep well. But, O Pīkoi, I beg you to wake at dawn to kill my enemies. When full daylight comes they will be gone."

"I shall wake in time," Pīkoi answered as he pulled the *kapa* covers over him. He was tired and slept soundly.

But the chief could not sleep. Every little while he got up and went to the doorway of the sleeping house. The night was very black.

Dawn at last. Now was the time, the only time to kill those birds! In a little while they would be gone. But Pīkoi was sleeping soundly. The chief did not know what to do. He said he would wake in time, the chief thought, but he does not wake. Shall I call him? No. He is the son-in-law of Keawenui, too great a man to anger. I dare not wake him. The chief went to the doorway again. With heavy heart he watched the daylight grow.

The sun was shining when Pīkoi awoke. He greeted the chief. "Have you been out to look for your birds?" he asked.

"It is too late," the chief answered sadly. "You slept soundly and now the birds are gone."

"Go out and look," said Pīkoi. "Look in your sweet potato patch."

The chief went. He found the dead birds. "Dead!" he cried joyfully. "My enemies are dead! But what could have killed them?" He stooped to look. "Shot! But who—?" Suddenly he knew! He hurried back and met Pīkoi outside the sleeping house.

"They are dead!" the chief cried in excitement. "O my friend, I don't know when you did it. But you have killed my enemies! My people will have food!"

❦ ❦ ❦

The chief of Puna offered Pīkoi canoes to finish his journey. "Good!" Pīkoi said. "The trails are rough and long." He and his young men paddled. As they went along the coast they stopped at villages, they climbed the mountain slopes, they looked at the great lava flows and listened to those who had seen Pele coasting down the mountainside on her fiery sled.

One day they stopped for water. "You are welcome to the water which flows from our springs," the people said. "But the springs are on the edge of the ocean and the water is a little salty."

"Let us get water from the mountainside," said Pīkoi.

"There is no spring on all the mountainside," the people answered.

Pīkoi looked long at the mountain. "Do you see that place where fog rests? Just above it is a spring."

"Not so," the men of the village told him. "We have climbed all over that mountain slope. There is no spring."

"You two," Pīkoi said to two of his young men, "climb to that place. Take two men of the village with you and take water gourds. Watch my arrow, for where it strikes the earth, there is the spring."

The men of the village did not want to go. "A long climb for nothing," they said.

"Pīkoi is wonderful," his young men answered. "He has shot rats so far away we could not see them. He shot birds in the dark."

"Yes, rats and birds a man may shoot, but no one can shoot a spring where there is no spring!" At last, however, two men said they would go.

The four climbed to the place where fog rested on the mountain, then they turned to look below. They saw Pīkoi raise his arms to shoot. They heard the arrow strike the earth above them. In a moment they had reached the place. There was the arrow sticking in dry earth.

"What did we tell you!" said the two from the village. Pīkoi's young men pulled out the arrow and water flowed—cool, clear water. The men of the village stared in wonder as the others filled their gourds. Then they ran down the mountain. "Water!" they shouted. "A good spring that flows freely. Bring your water gourds!" The whole village climbed to see the wonder and to drink the good water of the spring.

Water still flows from that mountain spring and when children stop to drink they hear, again, the story of Pīkoi.

The canoes went on. Often the men stopped to feast with a chief or to see the sights of a district. "A large island!" Pīkoi said. In his heart he longed to be at home, to see his young wife.

Then a runner came. "The high chief has come to Waipiʻo," he told Pīkoi. "The young chiefess sent me to tell you."

They reached Kohala and had not far to go. They paddled steadily. Pīkoi was watching the mountainside. "See that cloud of dust," he said. "There is a lizard— a great lizard."

"Yes," one of his young men said, "I have heard of that lizard. A great mother lizard and her children live on this mountain. The people fear them and never climb the slope."

Pīkoi laughed. "The lizard is large, that is true," he said, "but she will not kill men. Look!" he exclaimed as he made ready bow and arrow. "I shall shoot the lizard and then one of you climb up and get my arrow."

The young men looked at each other. "But the lizard's children!" they said. They did not want to meet those lizards.

"I shall kill them all," Pīkoi promised. "My arrow will go through the mother lizard. It will tangle the tails of the children and kill them too.

"Watch! I shall shoot. If you see little dust clouds running here and there you will know the children have escaped. But that is not what you will see. You will see one cloud of dust rise straight up. Then you will know that all are dead."

The young men watched as Pīkoi stood up in the canoe balancing himself. They saw him aim and heard him chant:

> "I am Pīkoi.
> Hush! Be still!
> There is an enemy on the mountainside.
> I shall have fun with that enemy.
> Large lizards! Small lizards!
> I shall kill all!
> Death to the mother!
> Death to the children too!"

The men watched the arrow fly and saw a single cloud of dust rise upward.

"I will go for your arrow!" every young man cried.

"I am not afraid."

"Let me get your arrow, Pīkoi!"

Pīkoi chose four to go. Soon they were back with the arrow. "It was just as you said," they told him. "Your arrow went through the mother and tangled the tails of the children, killing every one. We have told the villagers. Already they are climbing the mountain to see the dead lizards."

🐛 🐛 🐛

The people of Waipi'o had heard much of Pīkoi. They had heard of his killing of the bad-luck birds. They knew he was the husband of their beloved young chiefess and son-in-law of Keawenui, their great high chief. They had heard that Pīkoi and his young men were coming by canoe and they had set watchers to tell them when he came.

Now word went through the valley, "Pīkoi is coming!" A crowd gathered at the landing place. As Pīkoi's canoe came close, men waded out to meet it. Strong men lifted the canoe and carried it into the canoe shed. Only then did Pīkoi and his paddlers step out to be welcomed by the crowd.

Pīkoi went before Keawenui with greeting and with thanks. He found his wife. They wept with joy to be together once more.

"I have seen Hawai'i," Pīkoi said, "and now I am at home."

Translated by Mary Kawena Pūku'i from a Hawaiian newspaper.

Pele

Pele

Pele, goddess of the volcano, came with her brothers and sisters seeking a home in *Hawai'i-nei*. She tried island after island but always, as she dug her fire pits, she heard the voice of the sea.

At last she dug a great pit high up on Kilauea, far above the ocean. There she tended her fires. Sometimes she lived in peace with her family about her, while the brothers fed the fire in the pit and the sisters made *lehua lei* or danced the *hula*. But sometimes Pele went about the island. Often she went among her people in the form of an old woman. If anyone was rude to her he would be punished. Often a whole countryside would be laid waste because of some rude word or scornful laughter. There are many stories about Pele, of both her cruelty and her kindness, some very old and some of recent growth. Here are a few.

How Hawai'i Was Made Safe

Hi'iaka was Pele's youngest sister. She was beautiful and brave and Pele loved her dearly. But Hi'iaka was very different from Pele. The goddess of the volcano liked to destroy but Hi'iaka loved people and wanted to help them. She had young women companions from whom she learned to dance the *hula* and make *lei*.

From them she heard of the dangers which threatened people on her island of Hawai'i. She heard of giant *mo'o*, of man-eating sharks, of evil spirits and of a terrible whirlwind which destroyed homes and gardens of men.

"I shall go on a journey," Hiʻiaka said. "I shall travel around this island of Hawaiʻi and destroy these evil beings. I shall make Hawaiʻi a safe home for people. Who will come with me?"

Her sisters and brothers did not answer.

"I need a traveling companion," Hiʻiaka said again. "Come with me or I shall have no one to talk with but my shadow."

Still the brothers and sisters did not answer. As for Pele, she was stirring the fire in her pit and gave no thought to Hiʻiaka's words.

"Are you afraid?" Hiʻiaka asked the others. "Are you afraid to journey around your island of Hawaiʻi?"

"There are many dangers," one sister said.

"What are you?" Hiʻiaka asked. "Are you gods and goddesses or timid people?"

"We have no power against the evil beings who rule Hawaiʻi. You also have no power against them. They will kill you, Hiʻiaka."

"Pele will give me power," the young goddess said.

> "O Pele," she cried,
> "Great goddess of the volcano,
> Give power to Hiʻiaka,
> Give power to your dearly loved sister.
> I go to meet the great *moʻo,*
> And spirits that live in the forest,
> Fierce sharks that live in the bays,
> The whirlwind that lives in the valley,
> Destroying all in its path.
> O Pele, I ask you for power.
> Give me power to end all these evils."

Suddenly Pele turned from the fire pit. "I have heard your prayer, O Hiʻiaka," she said. "This *pāʻu* has the power of lightening. Take it. And in your hour of need call for the help of the wind and storm. They will answer. Now go."

"Alone?" asked Hiʻiaka again. "It is no fun to talk to my shadow. It doesn't answer."

Then Pele called her own serving woman. "Go with my sister," she commanded and turned again to tend her fires.

❦   ❦   ❦

The two journeyed. Hiʻiaka sang with joy as they walked under *lehua* trees covered with blossoms. Then she was quiet, watching the birds gathering nectar from the blossoms.

Suddenly the serving woman whispered, "I hear the grunt of a pig! What is it, a pig of the land or a pig of the sea?"

"Both!" laughed Hiʻiaka softly. "You hear the grunt of a pig of the land and also the grunt of a pig fish. Someone is taking an offering to Pele."

A moment later a young woman appeared. She was carrying a striped pig fish and a small struggling black pig.

"Greeting to you, Woman-in-Green," said Hiʻiaka.

The young woman gazed at her, wondering at her beauty. "Who are you?" she asked in a low voice. "O Beautiful One, who are you? And where are you going?"

Hiʻiaka answered the second question. "We go on a long, hard journey. We go through a dangerous forest, beyond the waters of Hilo, over the cliffs and beside the sea until we reach Kohala."

There was love in the eyes of the young woman as she said, "Let me go with you on that long, hard journey."

"Your offering is for Pele," Hiʻiaka made answer. "First take it to the fire pit, then return and journey with us."

Wonder and love had grown in the eyes of the woman as she looked and listened. "You, yourself, are Pele," she whispered as she fell on her face before Hi'iaka. "O Beautiful Goddess, accept my offering."

"No, I am not Pele. She lives above in the fire pit. Go to her there, but make no mistake. You will see tall and beautiful women. Those are sisters and servants of Pele. Look for an old woman. Look for one lying on mats close to the fire. You will find her well wrapped in *kapa* and stirring the fire with her long stick. Give your offering to her and to no else, for that old woman is Pele. Go quickly."

But the woman did not go. "My offering is for Pele," she said, "but you, O Beautiful Goddess, for you I have great love. If I leave you I shall never find you again."

"I promise that my companion and I will wait for you," Hi'iaka told her. "You will find us here among the *lehua.* Go."

So Woman-in-Green went to the fire pit and, after leaving her offering, returned to the *lehua* trees, ready to journey with Hi'iaka. The three went on all day, wading streams and climbing the steep sides of valleys. The sun set. "Let us find some house where we can spend the night," the serving woman said.

"No," Hi'iaka answered. "Travelers must sleep in the open." So each wrapped herself in her *kapa* and slept under the trees.

Hi'iaka was awake at dawn. "Listen!" she whispered. "Voices!"

As the light grew the voices came nearer. Soon the three saw a company of girls who had come from a nearby village. They were gathering *lehua* blossoms and making *lei*. One girl ran to Hi'iaka. "Friendship to you!" she cried, as she threw a *lei* about Hi'iaka's shoulders. All the girls crowded around the three travelers and made them welcome. "Come home with us and eat," they said.

It was pleasant to rest, to eat good food and enjoy song and *hula*. But Hiʻiaka was eager to journey farther. "We are travelers through Puna," she said, "tell us about the trail."

"Take this trail," the girls answered, pointing to a well-worn path that led by the edge of the sea.

"The sun is hot on that trail," Hiʻiaka said, "and the way is long. We love the shade of the forest. Is there no forest path?"

"Oh no!" the girls told her. "You must go by the edge of the sea."

"There must be a path through the forest," Hiʻiaka insisted.

"Long ago there was a forest trail," one girl answered, speaking in a whisper, "but no longer do we travel through the forest for there is great danger."

"What danger?" asked Hiʻiaka. "Shall we trip on vines or fallen logs? Must we wade rocky streams?"

"This beautiful forest belongs to Panaʻewa, the great *moʻo.*" The girls looked anxiously toward the forest and their voices were full of fear. "If anyone dares to enter, the servants of the great *moʻo* make ready his *imu*. Fog gathers about that unlucky one. As he wanders, lost, he is attacked by wind and icy rain. He is struck by a falling branch or tripped by a twisting vine so that he falls over the cliff. Never again will he see the sunlight."

"The great *moʻo!*" Hiʻiaka cried. "I am here to conquer him! Come, my companions. Let us take the forest path."

Her companions felt the courage of the young goddess. They knew that she was protected by the power of Pele. "The forest path!" they cried.

The company of girls who had been so happy a few moments before were all weeping now. "Do not go," they begged. "You are too beautiful to be cooked in the *imu* of the great *moʻo,*" and they tried to hold Hiʻiaka back.

Laughing she broke from them and the three entered the forest of the *mo'o*.

Hiʻiaka entered the forest fearlessly but she knew there was danger. She watched every tree and stump. She listened to every sound. The trail was very old and dim. The girls tripped over vines. They climbed over logs and waded streams. Always they watched. Darkness fell. "Lie here and sleep, for you are weary," Hiʻiaka said. "I shall stay awake."

Through the long night the young goddess watched and listened. The darkness was deep about them and the night was very still. Danger must be all around, but Hiʻiaka could neither see nor hear it.

In the faint light of dawn she saw a little bird high among the trees. It was gathering nectar from the *lehua* blossoms. "O little bird," she said under her breath, "are you a messenger sent by the great *mo'o*? You gather nectar from the blossoms. Are you telling me to drink *'awa* and sleep?"

The bird flew away. It must have carried its message to the giant *mo'o* for suddenly Hiʻiaka heard a terrible voice chanting through the forest,

> "Food! Here is food!
> Make ready the *imu!*"

Hiʻiaka's companions sprang up from their sleep. "That voice!" they whispered. "That terrible voice!"

"A terrible voice!" Hiʻiaka repeated, and her words rang bravely through the forest. "But it is only a voice!"

Her shout was like a signal for attack. Fog came from every side, seeking to choke the three with its cold fingers, blinding them and wrapping them in shoulder capes of mist. "Keep close behind me!" Hiʻiaka called to her companions. "We must not lose each other," and she drove back the fog with the sacred *pāʻū* of Pele.

Then came cold rain and bitter wind. Branches fell about the three and vines twisted around their feet. Hundreds of little forest birds came screaming and dashed themselves against Hiʻiaka and her companions. But the goddess whirled her wonderful *pāʻū* and drove her enemy deeper into the forest. For a moment she could rest. As she rested she shouted a chant to her enemy:

> "O Panaʻewa, bitter is the storm.
> Branches rattle about us,
> Leaves and flowers are falling.
> This is the growl of the *moʻo,*
> The *moʻo* stirred by his anger!
> O Panaʻewa,
> I strike you!
> I strike with my powerful *pāʻū!*"

Panaʻewa heard her shout and sent his *moʻo* army. They dashed through the forest, leaping from rocks, hiding behind bushes, then jumping out with open mouths and gleaming teeth.

But Hiʻiaka whirled her sacred *pāʻū.* She struck at the *moʻo* army, killing and wounding. Fearlessly her companions fought on either side. There was snapping of jaws and swinging of blows until darkness fell.

Night came at last. All about lay the bodies of dead *moʻo.* Silence came after the roar of battle. "Sleep," the serving woman told Hiʻiaka. "Tonight you must rest and I shall watch." And Hiʻiaka slept.

Messenger birds went to the giant *moʻo.* "What news?" he asked them. "My *imu* is hot. Where are these women that I may cook and feast?"

"The women sleep," the messengers answered, "but our companions sleep in death. Those who went forth to fight lie dead, all except a few who took the form of trees."

The giant *mo'o* was angry. He called all his servants who still lived and this time gave his orders in secret. Each *mo'o* was to take the form of a tree or bush. They were to surround the sleeping women and crush them with their power.

But the serving woman did not sleep. At dawn there was no roaring voice but a low murmur through the forest. It seemed to come from every side. It seemed as if a light morning wind stirred the tree tops. But there was evil in the sound. The serving woman shouted a prayer:

> "O clouds, pour down your rain!
> Let your lightening flame!
> Your thunders crash!
> O Pele, great Pele,
> Show your power!
> Send forth your voice like a war drum!"

Pele heard and sent her storm clouds to help Hi'iaka. The giant *mo'o* and his servants came in the form of trees and bushes until they surrounded the women. Soon these trees and bushes felt vines climbing over them and holding them so that they could neither move nor strike.

Then they heard a mighty war call. It was as if the wind itself blew a great shell trumpet. This was followed by booming, as of a mighty war drum. Suddenly all the forces of Pele were let loose. Lightening flashed from the clouds, thunder roared, rain and hail fell until a great flood poured through the forest. The *mo'o* trees were uprooted and carried to the sea. The forest was swept clean of evil. Only a few twisted forms at the edge of the sea were left to remind the people of the evil that had once been there.

Hi'iaka looked over the windswept, rainswept woodland. She was thankful that she had won her first great battle. "This forest is safe now," she said. "Let us go on our way."

❦ ❦ ❦

Now the trail was even harder to follow than before, for the storm had uprooted trees and scattered vines. Tired and hot, the young women suddenly found themselves at the top of a cliff overlooking the sea.

"Here the trail is broken," the serving woman said. "Part has fallen into that deep bay."

"We can swim in the bay!" said Woman-in-Green quickly. "We are hot and tired. Let us jump into the bay and swim to the sandy beach on the other side."

"Good!" the serving woman answered. "Ready! I'll race you to the beach!"

"No!" Hi‘iaka's voice rang out sharply. Her companions, ready to jump, looked at her in surprise. "A terrible shark lives in that bay," the goddess told them. "He hides now at the foot of the cliff."

"You are mistaken," said Woman-in-Green. "See how the waves rush in. That whirlpool at the foot of the cliffs is made by the waves. We shall jump over it and swim to the beach." She turned to the serving woman. "Let us race."

"No!" Hi‘iaka cried again. "I tell you a terrible shark waits in the shadow of the cliff. Watch!" She broke a stalk of *kī* and peeled off the bark. "Watch this white stick," she said. "You can see it in the shadow. It is shark bait. You will see it seized and drawn under." She threw the stick. In a moment it had disappeared.

"It was covered by seaweed," said Woman-in-Green, "or carried down in the whirlpool. We two are not afraid." Again the two made ready to jump.

"Wait!" Hi‘iaka's voice rang out sternly. She peeled another stick. "Watch this! If this white stick floats I too shall swim with you." She threw it. A great shark's head rose from the dark water. The teeth gleamed as they seized the stick.

Hiʻiaka, ready for battle, whirled her sacred *pāʻū*. The great jaws snapped at her. The tail dashed waves against the cliff but Hiʻiaka was unharmed. Again she whirled her *pāʻū*. The shark floated dead, and the waves carried his body out to sea.

"Now we can swim," said Hiʻiaka. "This bay is safe for all."

🐋 🐋 🐋

"Tell us of the trail to Hilo." The three companions stopped before a small house and asked the way of the old people resting in its shade. "We want to go to Hilo," Hiʻiaka said again. "Are we on the right trail?"

"Yes, follow that trail," the old people answered. "Soon you will come to the Wailuku River. Two logs make a bridge over the river. But do not cross until you have made offering to the gods who guard the bridge."

"Gods?" asked Hiʻiaka.

"Yes, two powerful gods live there in a cave. The logs belong to them. When we want to cross we lay food on the logs—vegetable food or fish. If the gods are pleased they hold the logs firm and we cross safely."

"We have no food," Hiʻiaka said. "We shall make no offering. What then?"

"Then do not try to cross, for the gods will turn these logs beneath your feet and you will fall into the raging river. You will be dashed to death upon the rocks."

Hiʻiaka said no more and the three walked on. Soon they came to the river and the bridge of logs.

"Here is Hiʻiaka!" called a voice from a great cave. "She is one of our family—a goddess."

"She may be one of our family," said another voice, "but I am hungry. Let her pay to cross. Bring an offering of food, O Hi'iaka. Make offering to the gods for a safe crossing."

"Gods!" shouted Hi'iaka angrily. "You are no gods! We have no food for you!"

By this time people had gathered on each side of the river. "They are indeed gods," these people cried. "We never try to cross without making offering."

"I'll show you they are no gods!" shouted Hi'iaka as she whirled her *pā'ū*. The people saw two frightened figures rushing away to hide in a cave far up the river. Hi'iaka followed them and the two dashed out to find another hiding place. The *pā'ū* of the goddess flashed and the figures were turned to stone.

Hi'iaka returned to the people. "The crossing is safe," she said.

Thankfully people followed the three companions into the village. They set food before them and hung sweet smelling *lei* about their necks. "We have long feared those evil ones," they said. "Now you have given us safe crossing."

❦ ❦ ❦

In Waipi'o Valley lived a terrible whirlwind. When he saw Hi'iaka coming he threw a cloud of dust about her, then rushed away to the head of the valley.

Hi'iaka and her companions followed. The goddess whirled her *pā'ū* and struck. But her enemy swept away, darted behind her and attacked. Again and again she struck, but her enemy twisted away. He threw great trees at her and covered her with dust. Hi'iaka struck and struck again, but her *pā'ū* never touched her enemy.

At last he drew into a mountain cave to rest. Hi'iaka stood panting. This battle was by far the worst because her *pāʻū* could never find its mark. Now at last she called upon her mighty sister:

> "Pele, O Pele,
> Great goddess of fire,
> Listen to Hiʻiaka—
> To your dearly loved sister
> Who fights in Waipiʻo,
> Who battles the terrible whirlwind.
> See how he twists and he hides.
> My *pāʻū* never can reach him."

Pele, far away in her fire pit, heard and sent help. Dark storm clouds gathered above the valley and lightening flashed from cloud to cloud—the lightening of Pele's anger. Thunder roared. Then rain fell—rain and hail. They struck the whirlwind.

He crept back into a far corner of his cave. He was not dead, but his power was broken. Never again would he destroy homes and gardens of men. Waipiʻo became a fair and peaceful valley.

Hiʻiaka's journey had indeed made Hawaiʻi a safe home for the people.

From Pele and Hiiaka *by Emerson and*
Hawaiian Legends of Volcanoes *by Westervelt.*

How Hawai'i Was Divided

Pele lay watching her fires while, about her, her sisters sat making *lei* of *lehua*. "Look!" one whispered, "see that handsome man!"

A handsome man, indeed, stood on the point of rock above the edge of the pit. He smiled down at the women and chanted:

> "O beautiful women,
> Making *lei!*
> You shall make them.
> I shall wear them.
> *Aloha!* My greetings to you!"

The sisters were delighted. "Look, Pele!" they whispered again. "See that handsome man. Let us invite him to come down. Let us hang our many *lei* about his neck."

"Handsome man!" said Pele scornfully. "That is a pig! It is Kamapua'a, the pig!"

"Oh no, you are mistaken!" the sisters told her. "You have not looked at him. We know pigs. We have seen them often in the lowland. We know the shape of a pig, the head of a pig, the snout of a pig. This is no pig, we tell you. Look, Pele, look!"

"You do not recognize me, O Pele," the young man called. "Invite me to come down that we may know each other."

"Oh, I know you quite well!" Pele answered. "Pig with a long snout! Pig with a wagging tail! I recognize you!"

The young man was indeed Kamapua'a, the pig god. Pele's true words angered him.

> "Red-eyed Pele!" he chanted,
> "Woman with eyes like the *noni*-dyed *kapa!*
> Woman who sends rain on the lowlands—
> Black rain of rocks and hot lava!"

Now Pele, too, was angry. "Stir up my fires!" she commanded her brothers. "Let this pig feel the black rain and hot lava. We shall drive him from this island. Hawai'i is ours! Let the pig return to O'ahu."

The fires blazed in the pit and hot lava overflowed. Dark clouds gathered, lightning shot from cloud to cloud and thunder roared. The earth shook. Pele could no longer see Kamapua'a, but she heard his scornful voice chanting:

"The fire of Pele
Is burning the uplands of Puna.
Black smoke darkens the heaven.
It falls on the snow of the mountain.
The roll of thunder is heard—
The loud voice of Pele, the woman.
The pit is filled with the fire
And smoke of Pele, the woman."

So! He still lived! Pele stamped on the floor of the fire pit. Lava burst forth once more and filled the pit, hot rocks shot upward, steam and smoke rose until it seemed as if earth and heaven were afire. Surely Kamapua'a was burned! Pele listened and heard no scornful chant. The pig god was dead! "Let the fires die down," she commanded.

🐗 🐗 🐗

Slowly the fire died. Lava turned black and no longer flowed, smoke disappeared and the sky became clear. And there, in the light of the sun, Kamapua'a stood on the same point of rock! Pele had neither killed him nor driven him away.

"Rekindle my fires!" she shouted. Again Kīlauea was filled with fire and lava.

And now Kamapua'a prayed:

"O gods of the skies!
Let the rain come. Let it fall.
O clouds in the skies, black as smoke,
Let the heavens fall on the earth,
Let the heavens roll open for the rain.
Let the storm come!"

Rain poured from heaven. It hissed upon the hot lava and rose in clouds of steam. Great waves rolled in from the sea and poured over the island. The crater was filled with water and the fires of Pele were out. Kamapua'a still stood upon the point of rock and laughed, for he thought he had conquered Pele.

But the fire-making sticks had been hidden away where no water could touch them. "Rekindle the fire!" Pele commanded and her brother set to work.

Kamapua'a watched the rubbing, rubbing of the fire stick in the soft wood. Smoke rose. Soon fire would follow. "Let us be friends, O Pele," he said.

"Yes, Pele," her sisters and brothers begged. "It was you who started this quarrel. You called Kamapua'a a pig and made him angry. You have not driven him out. He cannot destroy you nor can you destroy him. Make peace or between you the island will be laid waste."

"Yes," Pele said at last, "I started the quarrel. Fire and water! Neither is stronger than the other. Let us make peace, O Kamapua'a."

So peace was made and Hawai'i was divided. Pele still sends her lava flows over Ka'ū, Puna and Kona, but the other side of the island belongs to Kamapua'a. There rain falls and forests and gardens grow. "Never fear that lava will reach Hilo," people say. "Hilo is safe. This side of the island does not belong to Pele."

From Hawaiian Antiquities and Folklore *by Fornander.*

Hōlua Sledding

"'*Ā! 'Ā*, Kahawali!" The shouts rang in the man's ears as he climbed the hill.

Kahawali was a *hula* master. There had been weeks of prayer and hard work as he taught young men and women the *hula* chants. He taught them the music and the gestures that go with each chant. Then had come the anxious time when his young people prepared for their graduation. They had given their *hula* before the chief of Puna and the chief had been pleased. Kahawali's pupils had done well and he was proud and happy over their work.

And now a time of rest and sport! His favorite sport—*hōlua* sledding. The crowd had come from the chief's home to watch. There were his young *hula* dancers. There were their parents and friends—a happy crowd dressed in new *kapa* and decked with *lei*. It was glorious to feel the flying sled beneath! Glorious to hear the shouts of the people!

Kahawali climbed, panting, to the hilltop and stopped to rest. His companion was there before him. "I did not go half so far as you," his companion said. "I never saw anyone so skillful with a *hōlua*."

"I have had long practice," Kahawali answered. "Are you ready? Then let us go once more."

With a running start Kahawali threw himself on his long narrow sled. Down the steep grassy slope he flew. A glorious feeling! This was the way a bird must feel when it swooped through the air. There were uneven places in the slide, but Kahawali's active body kept his balance. He reached the bottom and went far out on the grassy plain. Again he heard the shouts. The swift movement! The shouts of praise! Oh, it was glorious sport!

Again he climbed the steep hillside and reached the slide. He found an old woman beside his companion.

"This woman wants to race with you," his friend laughed. "I am lending her my *hōlua.*"

Kahawali looked at the old woman. Her eyes were bright but her body did not look strong. Did she know the dangers of the sport? "This slide is not easy," he said.

The old woman spoke grimly. "Let us race!" she answered. She threw herself on the sled more quickly than the men had thought possible. Down she went with Kahawali just behind.

But she had not his skill for the uneven places in the slide. Off she rolled and her sled went on alone. With great skill Kahawali passed the old woman without touching her. Again the glorious feeling of rushing down like a swooping bird! Again the shouts of the crowd! Shouts for him and laughter for the old woman! He hoped she had not hurt herself.

No, there she was back at the starting point. He stopped for her sled and carried both up the hillside. He put her sled beside her. "Better not try that again," he advised. "This trail is too steep for a beginner."

"Your sled is better," the old woman said. "Let me use yours."

"It is not the sled that is better, but the skill of the one who slides." Without another word Kahawali took a running start, threw himself on his *hōlua,* and started down once more.

He listened for the shouts of the crowd. But instead of shouts of praise he heard cries of fear! As he slid on the plain he saw people running. They were crying out as if some danger followed. Kahawali turned to look. The old woman was coming down the slide on a *hōlua* of fiery lava. The earth shook beneath her and lightning flashed above. Pele! It was Pele to whom he had refused the sled! Pele laughed at the crowd!

The angry goddess was halfway down the slide. Kahawali snatched up his spear, which he had stuck in

the ground, and ran. All about him he heard frightened cries. Behind him came the roar and hiss of flowing lava. He ran toward the sea, for there was safety.

Kahawali was as skillful at running as at other sports. He was ahead of the crowd with the ocean not far away. Suddenly he came to a narrow gulch. There was no time to go around, no time to climb down and out again. Quick as thought Kahawali bridged the gulch with his long spear, ran across on it, picked up his spear and ran on. The lava was close behind. It filled the gulch and overflowed to follow Kahawali.

But now Kahawali was near the ocean. He saw a fishing canoe close to shore. His brother's canoe! "Wait!" Kahawali shouted. "Take me with you!"

He waded into the water and climbed into the canoe. His brother paddled with all his strength, but Kahawali set up his spear and it became both mast and sail. The storm wind pushed against it and carried the canoe to safety.

But those who had laughed at the old woman were caught by the lava flow and turned to stone. There they may be seen today—stone people fleeing across the Puna plain.

From Hawaiian Folk Tales *by Thrum.*

The Puna Chief Who Boasted

There was once a Puna chief who could talk of nothing but his own district. Wherever he went he boasted of Puna.

"Beautiful Puna," he chanted.
"Its fields and its gardens are shining
Like a mat spread over the hillside
And edged above by the forest."

"Be careful," people warned him. "Remember Pele! That goddess does not like boasting!"

"I fear her not!" the chief answered. "She lives above in the pit, tending her fires. Puna is safe from her evil." And he went on boasting:

"My country is beautiful Puna,
Land where all food plants are growing,
Land where bananas hang heavy,
Where potatoes burst from the earth,
Where sugarcane stalks are the sweetest.
My country is sweet-smelling Puna.
To the seaman who comes near our coast
The winds bear the fragrance of *hala*.
Birds gather over our trees
Drinking the nectar of blossoms.
My country is beautiful Puna."

A wise *kahuna* heard these words. "Alas!" he said. "Your boasting has angered Pele. Return to your country. You will find its beauty laid waste."

"Ho!" shouted the chief. "I do not fear your words! No harm can come to Puna!" But for all his shouting the chief was frightened. As quickly as wind and paddle could take him, he returned. He reached a point of land, beached his canoe, climbed a hillside and looked toward his beautiful Puna.

Black smoke hung heavy over all his land. As he looked, wind lifted the smoke and he saw no fertile fields and gardens, but a waste of twisted lava. No flowers bloomed in the forest, only spurts of flame. No fragrance of *hala* was borne on the wind, but the bitter smell of smoke.

Pele had been angered by the chief's boastful words. Now he knew that no land below her fire pit was safe from her power.

From Hawaiian Legends of Volcanoes *by Westervelt.*

The Girl Who Gave Breadfruit

"Our breadfruit must be done."

"They smell as if they were roasted. Let us look." The two girls bent over the coals in which they were cooking the breadfruit they had gathered.

"That one looks well roasted," said the older girl, uncovering it with her stick. "I love cooking on the mountainside, all by ourselves! I can hardly wait for the food to cool, I am so hungry! I'm sure this is done," and she lifted one blackened breadfruit with the point of her stick.

The younger girl had been looking down the trail. "There is an old woman down there," she said. "Poor thing! She is lame. I'd better go and help her climb this hill."

"Oh, don't bother! She is no relative of yours! Why help a stranger? Anyway she is probably going to take the lower trail."

"Yes," the younger girl said, watching, "I think she has taken the lower trail, but I always feel sorry for old people who are alone. I think how it would be if my grandmother had none to help her."

"Look!" said her friend. "This breadfruit is done. It is ready to fall apart. We must get them all out at once. Push off the coals, while I pull out the bread fruit. *Ē,* but they are hot!"

"Give me food. I have had nothing to eat all day." The girls were startled by the voice of the old woman who stood close beside them, watching them hungrily. She was frail and bent and leaned heavily on her walking stick.

The older girl glanced up. "We have not food for strangers!" she said. "We have only enough for ourselves and for our families. Ask your grandchildren for food!" and she went on opening a breadfruit that it might cool.

But the younger girl smiled up at the old woman. "Sit there," she said, pointing toward a rock, "while I prepare the food." She laid half a breadfruit on a large leaf. It was golden brown inside and looked and smelled so good that the girl's mouth watered. She took it to the old woman, saying, "It is very hot. Be careful!" Then she prepared a piece for herself and all three ate.

The girls did not talk now, for they felt shy with the old woman sitting near them. Her breadfruit was soon eaten. "How can she eat the hot food so fast?" the younger girl wondered as she got up to offer another piece.

The older girl made signs to her not to give away any more. But the younger brought another large piece of golden breadfruit to the old woman.

The old one took it without a word. When it was gone she rose. She spoke only to the younger girl. "You have been well taught," she said, then started up the trail.

She was saying something which the girls could not hear. Suddenly she stopped and turned. She looked at the younger girl and her eyes were young and fiery. "There will be strange doings on this mountain side," she said. "Tell your family to hang bits of *kapa* about their home. Tell them to do this for ten days. So they shall be safe." She was gone.

"What a queer old woman!" the young girl said wonderingly.

"Crazy!" said her friend. "It is not wise to give food to every queer person you see. Some day you will get into trouble!"

The girls finished eating. They wrapped the food that was left in *kī* leaves and started home.

The younger girl told her family about the queer old woman. "My friend said she was crazy and I should not have given her food. But I thought of you, Grandmother. I did not want her to go hungry."

"You did right, child," the grandmother answered.

"The old have done hard work," the mother added. "When they can no longer work, others should feed them. I hope you gave the old woman all she wanted of your breadfruit."

"Yes, Mother. She ate much and very fast. Then she rose and started away. When she turned back her eyes gave me a fiery look, and she said these words: 'There will be strange doings on this mountainside. Tell your family to hang bits of *kapa* about their home. Tell them to do this for ten days. So they shall be safe.' Then she was gone."

The girl's parents looked at the grandmother and she looked at them. "We must obey at once," said the grandmother.

The mother went to fasten fluttering bits of *kapa* to the house. The grandmother turned to the girl. "That old woman was Pele," she said.

Seven days passed. Then one evening a neighbor came running. "Look!" he cried. "Pele is angry. She is stirring the fire pit on Mauna Loa."

The family ran out to see. Fire was shooting from the mountaintop. All the mountainside was lighted by that mighty torch. A cloud had gathered above the fire and in the cloud they saw a woman's form. She was very young and beautiful with streaming, fiery hair.

"Her eyes!" the girl said in wonder. "Her eyes are like the eyes of the old woman."

The next day there was no fiery torch. "But the lava is flowing," people said. "Somewhere it is flowing down the mountainside. Pele is sending her lava to destroy those who have made her angry."

In the afternoon a runner came from higher up the mountain. "The lava is coming this way!" he cried.

Everyone made offering to Pele. The young girl's father offered a bowl of *poi* and another of *'awa*. "Our

best offering has been made already," the grandmother told them. "No offering made now can turn aside the anger of Pele. She will punish those who have been unkind to her."

People waited. They looked and listened. Perhaps the lava flow had stopped.

No! There was a crackling in the forest above. Trees were burning. Then people saw a great black wall that rolled slowly down the mountainside. It flattened large trees and rolled over them. The family of the older girl ran from their house. Their mouths were open but the younger girl could not hear them scream. She heard only the crackling of fire and saw that terrible black wall roll over house and land. Frightened, she caught her grandmother's hand. "Let us run!" she cried. "That wall of lava is coming straight toward us."

But the grandmother was not afraid. "'They shall be safe,'" she said. "Those were the words of Pele who does not forget."

The girl saw a fiery crack in the black wall. Then the lava stream broke in two and flowed on each side of their home. Houses and gardens were on a little island of safety with a broad stream of hot lava on each side. The lava moved slowly past. At night it glowed as the cool black top cracked and showed it fiery hot below. As they watched it the family prayed, giving thanks to Pele that their home had been spared.

Told to Mary Kawena Pūkuʻi by her mother.

Kalapana

"*Aloha,* old man! Where are you from and why do you paddle to Puna?" The old man pulled his canoe up on the sand and stood panting. He was a queer figure, tall and bony, with long white hair tangled by the wind.

Tired from handling the canoe he could not speak at first. At last he said, "My name is Kalapana. I come from Kaua'i. All my life I have longed to see Pele, that great goddess of the volcano. I made a promise that, until I could see her, I would never cut my hair. There has been much to do, time has passed and now I am an old man. But the wish is still strong in my heart. I have kept my promise and at last I come to Hawai'i, the island of Pele."

The man of Puna looked at the old man's thin legs, then turned to glance at the mountain. "The trail is long," he said. "This day is nearly done. Come home with me, Kalapana, to rest and eat."

Very thankfully Kalapana followed his new friend. Rest and food were good! He slept until the sun was high the next morning. When he awoke he went at once to the door. "I must go!" he said. "I can hardly wait now that I have reached Hawai'i."

"Not today!" his friend answered. "Here the sun is bright but clouds lie thick in the upland. You would find fog and rain. The rocks would be slippery and you might lose the trail."

Impatiently the old man waited. He walked about the village and watched people at their work. He was greeted kindly, though some laughed at his long tangled hair. "It is a promise," his friend explained. "Long ago Kalapana promised he would never cut his hair until he had looked upon Pele, goddess of the fire pit."

"What if someone cut it for him?" one boy whispered to another.

The other looked at him questioningly. "Do we dare?" he whispered back.

Three days Kalapana waited. On the fourth his friend called him early. "The time has come," he said. "Today the sun shines even on the mountaintop. Here is food, for the trail is long. Start now while the day is cool. Be strong for the journey and may you have success!" He guided Kalapana on his way, showed him the trail and watched the old man till he became small in the distance.

For a time Kalapana climbed eagerly. Then, as the trail became steep and the sun hot, he went more slowly. He stopped in the shade of a small tree, ate a bit from his *kī*-leaf bundle and rested. Then he went on.

As he tramped steadily over old lava flows and across dry plains he thought of Pele, the beautiful goddess whom he was soon to see. The trail led up and up. The rocks had been hot under his feet but now they were cool. The sun no longer beat upon the old man and he was glad. Glancing up he saw a sheltering cloud. It was good to be out of the burning sun and he sat down to rest and catch his breath. Then he went on.

Suddenly rain! It poured about him like a waterfall. The old man slipped and fell. He got to his feet but could not find the trail. He tried to go on but the rain blinded him. It blew in his face and beat his body as if it meant to drive him back. At last, tired out, Kalapana gave up the struggle and started down. Now wind and rain were helping him. He found the trail and followed it.

The way was easy now and the rain had stopped. "I will finish my journey," the old man thought, though his body ached with the struggle. But when he turned he saw that the rain was still falling higher up the mountain. A wall of storm seemed to bar his way. Kalapana went back to the village by the sea.

Tired and weak after his climb and drenching, the old man was glad to rest for several days. Then, again, his friend said that Kīlauea was clear of rain clouds. Again the old man started.

This time he got far up the mountain. The climb was not so steep now and the trail led over old lava flows and around small craters. "I have almost reached her!" Kalapana thought. "Today my life's dream will come true. I shall see Pele!"

But again a storm struck him. Blinding rain drove him back. He tried to go on but could not. Tired out, at last he staggered down the trail.

"It is very strange," his friend said. "Here the sun has shone all day. It may be Pele does not want you to see her face. Come now, eat and rest."

Kalapana was too tired to eat. He threw himself upon the mats in the warm house and sleep came quickly. It was a sound sleep. The old man did not smell the aroma nor taste the flavors of the dinner meal. He did not hear the evening noises as people made ready for the night. In the silence that followed he did not hear the whispers of two boys or smell the odor of burning hair.

Toward morning he was wakened by hearing his name, "O Kalapana!" He opened his eyes and saw a woman standing by his mats. He could see her plainly— tall and more beautiful than any woman his eyes had ever looked upon. Her *pā'ū* was dyed red and she wore many *lei* of red *lehua*. Her eyes were very bright but they were kind. He knew that she was Pele and, in his joy, he could neither speak nor move.

"O Kalapana, I have come to you," the goddess said. "I did not want you to come to me in the fire pit. So I sent a storm to turn you back. But, O Kalapana, why have you cut your hair?"

He tried to say, "I have not cut it," but no words came. He raised his hand and felt his hair. He felt short ends and smelled the odor of burning. Someone had cut his hair—cut it with fire!

"I understand," Pele said, and her voice was kind. "It was not you who cut it, but some bad boys. Your punishment will not be great but, because your promise was not kept, you must not return to your own island. You must live and die in Puna."

Slowly the goddess disappeared. Kalapana lay quiet and content. He had seen Pele! It did not matter that his hair was gone for she understood the reason. She had come to him and he had seen her loveliness!

In the morning he told his friend what had passed in the night. "If you are to stay in Puna you must live with me," the friend said. "You can care for my garden while I fish. Stay as my companion."

So Kalapana stayed. The boys wondered at his happiness. "I have seen Pele!" he said. "My life's dream has come true." He had forgotten about his hair.

The old man went quietly about the village. He cared for his friend's garden and helped the neighbors, playing with a baby or gathering shellfish and seaweed.

His face was always full of joy. "I have seen Pele!" he said often, and he told those who would listen how the goddess had stood by his mat and spoken to him.

People came to love and respect the old man and when he died they named their district for him— Kalapana.

Told to Mary Kawena Pūku'i by a Puna cousin.

The Pounded Water of Kekela

This is a story of the days of the Hawaiian kingdom, of the days when Kekela was chiefess of Kona and when the people of Hawai'i had learned from the missionaries about the God of the Christians.

An old woman sat in her cave with her *kapa* log before her. She spread her bark on the log and had her beater ready at her hand but she was not working. She felt faint and tired this morning and oh, so thirsty! She looked longingly at the little water in her coconut bowl but that was needed in *kapa* making.

She gazed out of her cave to the sunny mountainside. Dry grass, dry ferns and withering *lehua* trees—that was all she saw, for this was a time of drought in South Kona. Had it not been for a few deep wells everyone would have had to leave or die. As it was each family got only a little water. The old woman and her husband had divided their portion between them, then she had shared with their dog.

She glanced down at the dog, Huelani, lying beside her on the cool floor of the cave. As she looked he raised his head, but not to return her glance. Huelani was looking down the road and his tail began to thump in greeting.

The mistress's eyes followed his. She saw a young woman approaching, tall and beautiful, dressed in a red *holokū*. She wore a feather *lei* about her neck and from under her big *lauhala* hat floated hair that was soft and shining as the feathers of the *'ō'ō* bird. Her bare feet trod the rough lava road as lightly as if it had been a smooth floor. She was near the cave now and the old woman could see her plainly. The young woman must have seen the welcoming wag of Huelani's tail, for she smiled and beckoned to him. The dog sprang up and ran to her gladly, then flattened himself at her feet in great love and

devotion. She went on her way and, at a sign from her, Huelani followed.

All this the old woman had seen and she watched the two until they were out of sight. "Pele!" she whispered under her breath. "I have seen Pele!" And then, "Why did she take our dog?"

The old woman raised her *kapa* beater and began her work, deeply happy at what she had seen, yet sad at the loss of Huelani. Would he return or would Pele keep him?

The low afternoon sun slanted into the cave but the dog had not returned. Slowly the woman put away her things. Suddenly Huelani was beside her, shaking himself and splattering her with drops of water. "Huelani," the woman exclaimed, "you have found water!"

The dog capered proudly about the cave as if he knew he had made a great discovery. "Pele has brought water for her people," the mistress said softly, "and has shown it to you. I must hurry home to tell my husband."

Happy over her news, she waited impatiently for the coming of the old man. "I have news!" she said the moment he entered the house.

"What news?" he asked as he sat down heavily on the mats. He rested his head between his knees, so tired that he felt no interest in her words.

"It is news brought by our companion, Huelani."

"Well?" he muttered.

"He has found water!"

"That cannot be," the old man answered, raising his head. "There is no water for several miles."

"But he has found it," the wife said again. "Come with me tomorrow. We shall follow him and see."

But the husband would not come. "There is no water here," he said again. "In the time of my father, in the time of my grandfather, in all past years, no water has been known in this part of Kona."

So the woman and her dog went alone to the *kapa*-making cave next day. Huelani did not ask to share his mistress's drink. When they reached the cave he frolicked for a few minutes then darted off. She followed.

He was running far ahead of his mistress's slow steps but she saw him turn into the Road of the Lone Coconut. She followed until, not far from that single coconut tree, Huelani disappeared. "The cave!" she thought. "There is a cave near here." She found it and stooped down to peer in.

Water! A great pool of water disappearing in the darkness of the cave! There, beside the pool, stood her dog companion lapping thirstily. She had known he had found water but this great pool filled her with wonder and deep gratitude. She knelt there at the cave mouth and thanked God for this gift. Then she cupped her hand, dipped up water and tasted. It was fresh and good!

That day again she waited impatiently for her husband. "I myself have seen the water," she told him. "I have tasted it and found it fresh and good. Pele loves Kona and has brought us water."

The old man grunted. Tired with work in his dry garden, thirsty and discouraged, he gave little heed to his wife's words.

But next morning he consented to go with her to her *kapa*-making cave. "Wait till Huelani leaves," she said, "and follow him."

But Huelani did not go. He stretched out on the cave floor and closed his eyes as if he meant to sleep all day. "It is as I thought," the old man told his wife. "When people thirst they dream of water. You have had such a dream."

So the two argued and, while they talked, Huelani slipped away. "It doesn't matter," the old woman said. "Follow my directions. Walk to the place where the Lone

Coconut Road crosses this. Go *ma uka* on it. Near the tree is a great cave. There you will find our dog. Here, take these water gourds and fill them."

While he was gone the wife tried to work but was too excited. At last she saw him coming. From the way he carried the water gourds she knew that they were full.

He entered the cave and held out a gourd for her to drink. "Forgive me," he said. "I thought that you had dreamed but it is true. Pele has shown kindness to her thirsty people." Together the old couple knelt and gave thanks to God.

Then the husband spoke again. "Our chiefess must know of this." They started at once to Kekela's home on the shore.

They found her resting in the shade before her house. Kneeling, they went toward her. Kekela looked up and greeted them. "Why have you come?"

"You Highness," the old woman answered, "Pele has brought water for her people."

"What do you mean?"

"We have found it, for Pele showed the water to our dog. It is in the great cave near the Road of the Lone Coconut, just *ma uka* of the main road."

"That is news, indeed," the chiefess said, but they knew from her tone she did not quite believe it. "Rise," she told them, "for those who bring such news must not remain on their knees." Then she called servants, directed them to the cave, and bade them take water gourds to fill.

The old couple waited impatiently, seeing the doubt of the chiefess and her women and eager for the moment of joy. It came! The servants ran to the house and knelt before Kekela that she might taste the water. "The pool is large," they told her. "How large we cannot tell because the roof is very low and the cave dark."

"God is good," said the chiefess thankfully. She commanded that people gather *kukui* nuts for torches to light the cave while others gathered vines with which to measure the pool's size and the cave roof. The pool was found to be large, indeed, and fairly deep. There was water enough to last throughout the drought!

But the low roof of the cave made it difficult to reach. So the chiefess commanded that people bring wood. Everyone who passed that way must bring an armful. Those skilled in chipping stone were called. The wood was taken to the cave and a great crowd watched as men piled it on the cave roof and made a fire. When the fire died men chipped away the hot rock, using tools of hard stone. Another fire was built and more rock chipped away. After days of work a section of the cave roof had been removed and the pool was easy for thirsty folks to reach. It was named the Pounded Water of Kekela because of this pounding away of the roof.

Men, women and children came every day with water gourds. "It is the gift of Pele," they said thankfully. "She loves Kona and remembers her people when no rain falls." To the old couple and their dog the people gave great honor, saying, "they are the Chosen of Pele and she always chooses the best."

From Paradise of the Pacific, *Dec. 1933,*
a legend told by an old man of Kona,
and used by permission.

Other Legends
of the Island of Hawai‘i

Woman-of-the-Fire and Woman-of-the-Water

Long ago, not far from where the city of Hilo stands today, there lived two sisters. The older was chiefess of Hāla'i Hill. She had power over fire and was called Woman-of-the-Fire. The younger ruled over a smaller hill, Pu'u Honu. She had power over rain and was called Woman-of-the-Water.

Woman-of-the-Fire was a good chiefess. Her people worked hard. Some were farmers and some were fishermen. The women made mats and beat *kapa*. Hāla'i Hill was always full of busy work or merry games.

Then famine came. The gardens were dry and without food, the ocean seemed empty of fish, even the *kī* and fern of the mountain slopes shriveled and died. Woman-of-the-Fire shared her food with her people until that, too, was gone. Then she saw men and women grow pale and weak and heard the children cry for food.

She called the men together. "Be strong," she told them, "and do as I command you." To some of the men she said, "Gather wood—dry wood for a fire. We shall need much. Bring stones from the sea—good stones that can stand heat." To others she said, "Dig an *imu*. Make it broad and deep."

The men stared at their chiefess. Gather wood? Dig an *imu*? There was no food to cook! They wondered greatly but their chiefess was both kind and wise and had great power. They trusted her.

The wood was brought, stones gathered and a huge *imu* was made ready. The fire blazed until the stones were very hot. As the men cleared out the wood they wondered.

Now Woman-of-the-Fire walked slowly around the *imu*. They saw her point into it and heard her chant:

> "Here are sweet potatoes.
> *Kalo* is here,
> And here are bananas.
> Over there is pork
> And here is fish.
> Here are tender shoots of fern
> And over there is chicken."

Then she turned to her people. "I shall make an offering to the gods," she said. "Only so can you be fed. I shall go into the *imu*. Do not try to hold me back but cover me until no steam appears. On the third day you will see a cloud over our *imu*. It will be like a woman with a shining face. That is your sign. Uncover the *imu* and you will find food."

Woman-of-the-Fire went into the *imu* and her men covered her. Tears rolled down their faces for love of their good chiefess but they obeyed and covered her until they saw no steam. Then they watched beside the *imu*. With heavy hearts they watched for three long days.

"The cloud!" they cried. There, above the *imu,* was a shining cloud in the form of a beautiful woman. "It is the sign!" they said. Their hearts were full of fear as they took away the earth. What would they find?

They found the food the chiefess had named: sweet potatoes, pork and fish. There was food for men and food for women. The people were filled with joy and wonder as they spread a feast. "But our chiefess?" they questioned. "Where is she? Did she give her life to bring this food to us?"

Then they saw a woman coming from the shore. She was tall and beautiful and wore many *lei* of seaweed. The people stared. Suddenly a shout went up: "It is she! It is

our chiefess!" They went to meet her and fell on their faces before her, crying with joy.

"Come to the feast," she said. Woman-of-the-Fire ate among her people and told them of her visit to the gods. "They were pleased with my offering," she said. "They will bless your work and we shall have food in plenty."

After that the gardens grew well on Hāla'i Hill and the story of the chiefess's offering went through the country. It came to the ears of Woman-of-the-Water and she was angry. "All men praise my sister!" she said, "I, too, can win their praise."

So she did as Woman-of-the-Fire had done. She commanded her men to dig on *imu* on Pu'u Honu. She commanded them to gather wood and stones. She walked around the heated *imu* chanting, then entered it and told her men to cover her.

Her people waited hopefully. On the third day they saw, above the *imu,* a dark cloud in the form of a woman. "It is the sign!" they shouted and uncovered the *imu.*

But there was no food there, only the ashes of Woman-of-the-Water. Sadly they pushed back the earth.

Word of this came to Woman-of-the-Fire. "*Auē!*" she said. "My sister envied my power. Her power was great but different. She could have caused rain to fall on Pu'u Honu to make the gardens grow and bear much food. That I could not do. Instead she tried to do what I had done, though she had no power over fire. So she perished. *Auē! Auē!* Go bring her people here that we may share our food with them."

So all the people lived together on Hāla'i Hill. They left the great *imu* open. People still look at it and remember how Woman-of-the-Fire offered herself that her people might have life. There is no such crater on Pu'u Honu.

Told to Mary Kawena Pūku'i by an old lady of Hilo.

When the Ocean Covered Hawai'i

There was a time when men forgot the gods. They did not pray when planting *kalo* and sweet potatoes or give thanks when they gathered the vegetables for food. They did not pray before fishing or make thankful offering when the canoes returned well filled with fish. The walls of every *heiau* were broken and no *lei* of vines or gifts of food were left before the little figures which had once reminded men of their gods.

Among the servants of the chief of Waipi'o was a fisherman who worked early and long. Before sunrise he was at sea and when darkness fell he returned with a full canoe. Like others he had forgotten the gods. He did not pray to them for help or offer his first fish in thanks. Early and late he worked and it seemed to him his life was very hard. The fish he caught went to the household of the chief. There was little left for him and his wife.

One morning he had reached his fishing ground before the sun rose. He baited his hooks, dropped his line and waited. Did he feel a bite? He carefully pulled up the long line, coiling it so that it should not tangle. Only a bit of seaweed! He let down the line once more.

The sun rose over the ocean and all about him the water and sky were pink, pink as the inside of a shell, but the fisherman did not see the beauty. He was thinking only of his work. Was that a bite? Again he pulled up the line. The bait was gone from one hook but he had no fish.

So it went till the sun was high. For all his patient work and waiting the fisherman had—nothing! He was angry. "O you gods of the sea," he shouted, "you are not gods! You do not care that a poor fisherman works early and late. You do not care that the chief's men take all his catch. Today you send nothing to his hooks! Nothing! You do not care if the poor fisherman dies. I say you are not gods! If there are, indeed, gods in the sea then let me see you."

So the fisherman shouted in his anger. The answer came at once. The sky darkened. Waves rose foaming and suddenly, out of the rising waves, a shark appeared. He was a great blue shark. "The chief!" thought the frightened fisherman. "That is the shark chief, one of the ocean gods!"

In great fear he threw himself on his face in his canoe. He prayed to the shark chief to forgive his angry words. When he raised his head he saw the great fish slowly swimming around the canoe. At last the shark came close, lifted his head and spoke. "You think there are no gods! It seems that all men of Hawai'i think the same. The walls of every *heiau* are broken, no offerings are left for us—no *kalo* leaves, no fish, no 'awa and no bananas. The gods have waited long but no one prays, no one gives thanks. The people of Hawai'i are evil, evil! All shall be destroyed. The ocean shall roll over these islands and cover them."

The poor fisherman threw himself on his face again. "O Shark Chief," he prayed, "forget my evil words. I will pray to the gods each day. I will bring an offering of fish each night. I will tell men to rebuild the *heiau* walls and to remember the gods with prayer and offering. Only do not let this terrible flood come." Over and over the fisherman made his prayer.

At last he lifted his head. The shark chief was watching him and the shark's eyes did not look so cruel as before. "I have heard your prayer," he said. "Take your wife and climb to the highest mountain peak, for the flood will come. The word of the gods cannot be changed. Only, because of your earnest prayer, you two shall find safety above the flood." The shark disappeared under the waves.

The fisherman paddled to his own beach near the mouth of Waipiʻo Valley. He did not stop to pull his canoe high on the sand. That did not matter now. He ran to his wife and told her the shark chief's words.

"Let us go!" she said. She looked up to the top of Mauna Kea. "It is a long climb and we must start at once."

"Let us climb Mauna Loa," the fisherman answered. "That mountain, farther away, must be higher."

"I cannot walk so far," his wife replied, "and, Husband, the light of dawn is red on Mauna Kea while Mauna Loa is still dark. Surely Mauna Kea is the highest mountain in the world! Let us go there."

So they set off. They climbed over rough rocks and sharp grasses. They grew tired but did not stop to rest. They climbed on through darkness.

At last they reached the top. They looked about on their beautiful island and the woman chanted sadly:

> "O Hawaiʻi, my home,
> I shall see you no more!
> The many-colored sea will cover you—
> Will cover the houses of my friends,
> Will put out the cooking fires,
> Will cover the gardens and forests.
> No more will the *hula* drum be heard
> Or the shouts of the surfers.
> No more will men work in the fields.
> No more will they join in games and dancing.
> Only the sea will be left.
> The blue sea will cover Hawaiʻi."

The two wept bitterly until they slept.

They were awakened by a distant roaring. They looked over the ocean and saw a wall of water rushing

toward the island. They saw it rush over the beaches and into the valleys, carrying houses and trees before it. Another wave came and another. Now the waves were rising over the mountainside. Up and up the ocean rose. It came with a low roar and with terrible power.

At last it was as close as it had been to their home on the beach near Waipi'o. Only now the water was all about. The two were on an island of rock in the midst of rolling blue waves.

The ocean was not rising now. It was sunny, calm and very blue, yet it was terrible. What could two people do alone on a tiny rocky island? "Would that we had died!" they said and clung to each other for comfort.

At last, weak and very tired, they slept. Their sleep was sound and long and when they woke the ocean had gone back to its rightful place. There was all Hawai'i steaming in the sunshine. But now it was a barren island, swept clear of homes, of growing things and people.

Sadly the two went down the side of Mauna Kea. They found the beach where they had lived. They found shellfish and seafood for their food.

Each day they prayed, each day they offered to the gods the best of their poor food. They hung many *lei* of seaweed about the little figures of the gods that still stood on the rocks.

Many years passed and Hawai'i was once more a land of growing things, of home, of gardens and green forests. It was a land of happy people who thought often of their gods.

From More Hawaiian Folk Tales *by Thrum.*

Kila

"**O** my sons, one of you must voyage to Kahiki. That far land was once my home and I would send messengers to my people there. The journey is long and full of danger. Which of you will go?"

"I will go!"

"I am the one!"

"Let me go, O my father!" All five of Chief Moʻikeha's sons were eager for the journey.

"It is hard for me to choose among you," the father said. "Here is a test: each of you shall make a small canoe of *kī* leaf. Make it carefully, then come to the river and let me see whose canoe sails most truly before the wind."

Soon the five were at the river bank, each with his canoe. Moʻikeha waded into the broad, shallow river and sat on the lee side, knees wide apart. "Now start your canoes from windward," he said. "Let us see whose canoe can sail straight between my knees."

The oldest son was first. Quickly he launched his small canoe and sailed it straight toward his father. Then a gust of wind caught it and sent it past. Disappointed and angry the young man lifted his canoe from the water. He had failed!

The second son was ready. He placed his canoe with care and gave it a gentle push. Right into the current he pushed it and the *kī*-leaf canoe was caught and floated down the river. This young man too had failed.

The third and fourth did no better. Then it was the turn of Kila, the youngest brother. He had been watching the current and feeling the wind. Now he stood at the starting point holding his canoe in the water and letting

the gusts of wind go by. For a moment the wind was gentle and steady. In that steady wind the small canoe sailed straight between the father's knees.

Mo'ikeha's eyes shone with pride and joy. "You have won the test, Kila, my son," he said. "You shall voyage to Kahiki." He threw his arm over the shoulder of his youngest son and the two walked off together, planning the voyage.

The four brothers came slowly behind. "It is always so!" one said angrily.

"Yes, we might have known Kila would win! From birth he has been the best-loved son. Listen!" The brothers stopped to hear the plan of the oldest. Then they went to the garden for tassel-stalks of sugar cane and pointed these stalks with bamboo knives.

They were busy at this when they next saw Kila. "Come with us, O Kila," they called. "We go to play a game with darts of cane. Here is a dart for you. Come."

Kila joined them gladly but Mo'ikeha called him back. "Your brothers are angry because you are to voyage to Kahiki," he said in a low voice. "They may seek to do you harm. Do not be alone with them. While you are away their anger will cool."

When the stars were right Kila sailed. A wise *kahuna* was his guide, a strong paddler managed the canoe, dangers were met with wisdom and skill and when time had passed Kila returned.

He was a man now in every way. He talked of his far voyage but was not boastful. He had forgotten the brothers' jealousy, and, if they still felt anger toward him, they kept their anger hidden.

After a time Mo'ikeha, high chief of Kaua'i, died. To his wise *kahuna* he had spoken a last command, "Kila shall be high chief of Kaua'i in my place. After a time let him carry my bones back to Kahiki for I would have them rest there in that land I loved."

So Kila became high chief and his brothers appeared loyal to him. They were always ready to do his will and gave no sign of jealousy. As for the father's bones, those had been hidden in a cave on Hawai'i where they were to stay until Kila could take them to Kahiki.

🐦 🐦 🐦

One day the brothers came to Kila. "All goes well, O Chief," they said. "You rule wisely and all men are loyal. Has not the time come to fulfill the command of our father and take his bones to Kahiki, the land he loved?"

"The time has come," Kila replied.

"Then let us go with you to bring them from Hawai'i. We five will take a double canoe and strong paddlers. We will bring the bones back to Kaua'i. Then you shall voyage on alone with your men."

"You speak wisely," Kila answered, and went to tell the plan to his mother and aunt.

They had not forgotten the brothers' jealously of Kila. "Do not go with them," they warned the young chief. When they saw they could not hold him back they went to his brothers. "We too shall voyage to Hawai'i," they said. "We too shall bring the bones of Mo'ikeha from Hawai'i to Kaua'i."

"There will not be room," one young man answered.

"We shall ride on the platform that joins the canoes," the women said. "We shall be very quiet, for we know how to make a voyage." But the young men refused. The five brothers spread their mat sails and started for Hawai'i.

Days passed. Then four returned. Their hair was cut in sign of mourning and they wailed aloud. "What is it?" the aunt and mother asked. "Do you weep for your father? Where is Kila? Tell us quickly what has happened."

"It was a shark," the oldest answered. He could hardly speak for sorrow. "We had our father's bones in the canoe. As we rounded a point of Hawai'i a strong wind caught us and overturned the canoe. While we struggled in the water a shark attacked Kila."

"What then?" the mother cried. "What happened to my son?"

"It killed him, Mother. We all swam to his aid but before our very eyes the shark ate our brother!" The young man wept aloud.

"What of your father's bones?" the aunt asked.

"All lost! We swam to the aid of Kila, forgetting them. When at last we righted the canoe the bones were gone."

The mother and aunt wept bitterly for the young man they had loved. All Kaua'i wept for its high chief.

But Kila was not dead. When the canoe reached the beach of Waipi'o, on Hawai'i, Kila had been asleep. The brothers had gently carried him to the beach and left him, wrapped in *kapa,* out of reach of the waves.

Kila had wakened. Sleepily he had heard the grating of the canoe as it was launched. He had turned and stretched. When at last he stood up the canoe was out beyond the reef. Had his brothers called him and he not heard?

"*Ē!* Come back for me!" he shouted. They turned at his call. "Come back for me!" he called again.

"We will return for you," the oldest answered.

Kila watched the canoe as it was paddled away. It disappeared around a point of land and Kila waited. But the canoe did not return. Kila walked up and down the beach and strained his eyes over the ocean. Had some accident happened to his brothers? Or had they meant to leave him behind? He did not know.

Darkness came. Under the starlit sky Kila still watched but his brothers did not return. It was almost morning when the tired young chief fell asleep.

The sun was high when farmers of Waipi'o wakened Kila. They asked him who he was. He told them he had come in a canoe from Kaua'i and had somehow been left behind. They gave him food and told him to come and work for them.

So Kila, high chief of Kaua'i, became a servant. He worked in the *kalo* patches, digging, weeding or pulling *kalo*. He prepared food and heated the *imu*. He carried water and went into the forest for fire wood. For three years Kila worked as a servant in Waipi'o. Often, at night, he lay wondering about his brothers. Had they been drowned or had they meant to leave him? And what of his dear mother and his aunt? What of his island of Kaua'i?

Sometimes Kila climbed a steep cliff trail as he went to get wood from the forest above. He did not know that a rainbow hung above him—the sign of a chief. But that rainbow was seen by a wise *kahuna.* Some days it was not there. The *kahuna* watched and wondered.

"Lena has broken the *kapu!* He has eaten food meant for the gods. He shall die!"

Lena was the name that Kila went by in Waipi'o. He heard the shouts. He had eaten no sacred food! Perhaps it had been stolen by a dog. The young man knew that it was easy to throw blame on a servant, on a man who had neither father nor brothers to help him. In their anger the men might kill him. Quickly Kila slipped into the forest, not knowing where to go for safety.

Suddenly he knew! He had heard men talk of a place of refuge not far away. If he could reach that place no one could harm him. Kila ran through the forest. He hid in a cave to rest, then ran on. He thought he heard men following him.

At last he found the place of refuge and ran inside its wall. There he threw himself down, panting. The wise *kahuna* was in this place of refuge. He saw the tired young man and over him a rainbow. "That is the one!" he thought. "That is the rainbow I saw above the cliff! I must tell the chief."

So the *kahuna* went to the chief of Waipi'o. "O Heavenly One," he said, "may you live long! I have found a son for you. Many times I have seen a rainbow hanging over the cliff, but when I reached the place, no one was there. Today I saw the rainbow again within the place of refuge. It hung over a young servant who lay panting on the ground. I do not know the name of this young man, O Heavenly One. I do not know where he has come from. But the meaning of that rainbow is clear! This man is, himself, a chief. Oh, take him as your son!"

The chief of Waipi'o trusted this wise *kahuna*. He had longed for a son and now Lena became his son. The chief came to love him dearly. He saw that the young man was wise and made him overseer of Waipi'o.

During his three years as servant Kila, or Lena as he was called, had learned much of farming. He had seen that there were not enough farms in Waipi'o. In time of plenty, gardens were not cared for. Then came a dry time and everyone was hungry.

Now that he was overseer Lena made new farming laws. All men must make gardens and a large farm must be made for the chief. Every man must give certain days to work on the chief's farm. On certain days he must work in his own garden. Waterways must be dug to bring water to thirsty plants when no rain fell.

Lena went about among the farmers, showing them how to give food to their plants and how to soften the earth so it would hold moisture. The food plants of Waipi'o grew as never before.

And now came a dry time throughout the islands. Little rain fell, some springs dried up, streams were small and food plants died. A hungry time had come.

But not in Waipi'o! Because of the laws and teaching of Lena its gardens were filled with food. Soon men from other parts of Hawai'i were coming to Waipi'o to trade for food.

Time went on. Still the farms of Waipi'o were bearing well and people began to come from other islands. Even in Kaua'i people heard that there was plenty in one valley of the island of Hawai'i. "Let us send a double canoe to Waipi'o," said Kila's mother.

"Yes," the aunt added, "you young chiefs gather paddlers and go to Waipi'o. Take mats and nets to trade for food and return quickly that our people may not die."

But the young men thought of Kila left behind in Waipi'o. What if he were still alive? They did not want to go there and they made excuses. "The story of food in Waipi'o may not be true," they said. Their food must be gone by now so that it is useless for us to voyage to Waipi'o."

But the mother and aunt would not give up. They talked to one son and then another. "You are the chiefs," they said. "You must bring life to Kaua'i."

At last Kaialea, one of the brothers, said to himself, Kila cannot be alive. Surely there is no danger in going to that valley where we left him. Aloud he said. "I will go." He chose paddlers, filled a double canoe with trade goods and sailed for Hawai'i. The sea was calm and the canoe reached Waipi'o safely but there trouble met them.

The canoe was seized by men of the chief. "You have broken the *kapu*," they said to Kaialea. "Today it is forbidden that any canoe be seen upon the ocean. Come before the chief."

Kaialea tried to tell the men that he had come from Kaua'i and did not know of the *kapu*. Kaua'i was hungry and he had come for food. His canoe was filled with mats and nets to exchange for food.

But the men would not listen. "Tell all this to the chief," they said. Kaialea was afraid, for a strange chief might be very cruel. And always there was the thought of Kila. What if he still lived? And what if he should tell the chief of the great wrong his brothers had done him?

Kaialea was brought before the chief and stole a quick look at his face. The chief did not look cruel. But who was the one who stood beside him? Did that man look a little like Kila? Could it be—? Then Kaialea heard someone call that young man Lena, the chief's son. Kaialea drew a deep breath of relief. He was foolish to keep thinking of Kila who must have died long ago!

Kaialea answered the chief's questions clearly: "I am a chief of Kaua'i and have come to trade for food. I am very sorry that we broke the *kapu* but my men and I knew nothing of it. I pray for your forgiveness, O Heavenly One. We have brought mats and nets. O Heavenly One, I beg you give us food and let us return to our people, for they are hungry."

The chief turned to his son and Lena asked, "You have been here before?"

Does the young chief know that Kila was left in this valley years ago by brothers from Kaua'i? Kaialea wondered with fear in his heart. I will show him I was not one of those brothers. Then he answered boldly, "No, O Heavenly One, I have never before been to Hawai'i."

So my brothers meant to leave me behind! Kila thought. If some accident had happened Kaialea would have told the truth. He is ashamed and so he lies. Aloud Kila said, "Take the young man to the prison house."

Kaialea was filled with fear for he thought he would be put to death. He was put in a comfortable house and given sleeping mats and food. But he could neither sleep nor eat for fear of death. This is because we left Kila!

he thought. Yet how could anyone know that he was Kila's brother?

Kila kept Kaialea in prison because of the lie he had told, but he took pity on his people in Kaua'i and sent them a boatload of food. But, from the dishonesty of Kila's men, the food never reached his people. They waited long and at last word came, word sent by Kaialea's paddlers. The young chief was in prison, the message said, and was to be put to death.

The mother and aunt were filled with sorrow. "Kila is dead," they said. "Now Kaialea is to die. Let us go to Waipi'o. Let us tell the chief to take our lives instead of the life of the young man."

🐛 🐛 🐛

Kila saw a company being led before the chief. His three brothers! His mother and his aunt! He longed to take his mother in his arms. Tears filled his eyes. He walked alone down to the stream. There, where no one could see, he let the tears flow. Then he returned to the council of the chief.

His mother and brothers had explained who they were and the need of food. "We sent the young chief, my son," his mother said, "but he has not returned. If he has done wrong, oh, let us die in his place! My sister and I are old. We have not long to live. Take our lives, O Heavenly One, and let the young man return to his people in Kaua'i."

The chief turned to Kila. "What say you, Lena my son?"

Then Kila spoke to his mother. "Have you no other son?" he asked. "Have you only the three that we see here and the fourth who is in prison?"

He saw tears in his dear mother's eyes. "I had a younger son," she said in a low voice, "but he was killed in a battle with a shark. His brothers brought me word." Then her tears flowed.

Kila would no longer hold back his love. "O Mother," he said, "I am Kila. There was no battle with a shark. My brothers left me here because of jealousy. Here I worked as a servant until the chief made me his son." He tried to take his mother in his arms.

But she was filled with anger at his brothers. "They lied!" she cried. "They deserve to die, all four of them! They left you, perhaps to perish, and brought back a lie about you. Let your brothers die, O Kila!"

"Not so," said Kila gently. "O my mother, the gods have turned this evil deed to good. Because of what I learned Waipi'o is filled with food in famine time. You shall return, my mother. Your boat shall be filled with food and you return. You and my aunt shall rule Kaua'i."

"I must stay here. Here is my dear father and here my work. Waipi'o has become my land. As for my brothers, I forgive them. Let them return with you and let them rule Kaua'i when you are dead. This is the word of Kila."

The mother and aunt wept and the young men bowed their heads in shame. Kila's words were carried out. Food was taken to Kaua'i. The land prospered under the wise rule of the two women and then under Kila's brothers. As for Kila, he became chief of Waipi'o.

From Hawaiian Antiquities and Folklore *by Fornander.*

The Rescue of Hina

"He shall be tall and strong and wise. The gods will give him power." Old Uli was muttering to herself as she walked down the rocky trail to the village of Hilo. She came to the chief's home and was greeted by the serving women: "*Aloha,* Uli!"

"Greeting to you, old woman!"

"Why do you come? Have you heard that another grandchild is born, another son of the chiefess?"

Uli seemed not to hear. Without a look at the serving women, she entered a house. There on a pile of fine mats lay Hina, her daughter, chiefess of Hilo. Beside her a baby slept.

Hina opened her eyes. "Uli!" she exclaimed in surprise. "You are welcome. It is long since you left your home in the upland. Have you come to see my baby? You did not come when his brothers were born."

The old woman did not seem to hear her words. Tenderly she lifted the baby and held him against her breast. There was great love in her old eyes, love and pride and a look of wonder at what this child was to become. "I have come for the little stranger," was all she said.

Hina held out her arms. "He is too small," she answered. "You cannot take him from me now."

"I can care for him," the old woman replied. "This is no common child. He will grow tall and strong. And he will have wisdom and power—power that will make all men wonder. I must take him now and train him."

"But, Uli, what of my other sons?" Hina asked. "I have eleven fine sons. Are they not tall and strong and wise?"

Uli made no answer.

"What of Nīheu?" Hina asked again. "He is stronger than the others, for I have watched the boys at play. Nīheu can lift and wrestle like a son of the gods, and he is wise. He can look into the flames and tell of happenings far away."

"All that is true," the old woman replied, "but I tell you this one, Kana, will be stronger and wiser than Nīheu. He will have power from the gods. You shall see! The time will come when you are in great trouble and Kana, only, can rescue you."

Without another word the old woman left the house and took the trail, carrying the baby carefully. In her upland home she nursed him. When she worked in her garden the child lay on a mat near her, protected by a shelter of *lehua* and sweet-smelling *maile.*

When he became a boy he worked beside her. Kana knew no one but his grandmother. He loved the wrinkled bent old woman who was always kind to him. She gave him her wisdom and prayed to the gods that his strength and power should grow, day by day. So he reached young manhood.

The high chief of Moloka'i wanted to marry. "I must have the most beautiful woman in the islands for my wife," he said. He called his bird messengers. "Fly over all these islands," he commanded, "and bring me word of the loveliest woman, one who is perfect from the top of her head to the soles of her feet."

The birds flew in every direction. Soon they returned to Hā'upu, the hill on which the high chief lived. "We have found her," they said. "We have found the most beautiful woman in the world. She is lovely as the rising sun, and her hair shines as the feathers of the ʻōʻō bird. We have watched her as she swims and surfs among her women."

"It is well," said the chief. "I shall have this woman. Who is she?"

"She is Hina, chiefess of Hilo on Hawaiʻi."

"Make ready my canoe," the chief commanded. "On the night of the full moon I shall go to Hilo Bay, for it may be this beautiful woman will surf in the moonlight."

On the night of the full moon Hina and her women did indeed swim in Hilo Bay. They played tag, hiding behind rocks, then dashing out into the silver waves. They surfed. At last they rested on the sand, warming themselves at a fire they had built.

Hina left them there. "One more ride on a great wave," she called, and swam to the outer edge of the reef where the ocean waves broke on the coral.

She was tired from her swim and looked about for a rock where she might rest. She saw a shadow on the water. A rock! She swam to it, but found it was a canoe. Some fisherman, perhaps. "Come and rest before you surf to shore," a voice called, and friendly hands helped Hina into the canoe.

Gladly the chiefess sank down for a moment's rest. Someone threw a soft covering about shoulders. It felt like a feather cape. How strange! And this was a large double canoe! Hina was filled with wonder.

Suddenly she realized the canoe was moving. She felt the slap of ocean waves and, in the moonlight, saw the men working at the paddles. "Where are you taking me?" she asked. I must go back. My women will search for me and will be frightened. Take me back to Hilo."

"No, beautiful woman," a man answered gently. "I would make you my wife. You shall live in a home of many houses on Hāʻupu Hill. You shall have serving women in plenty. You shall listen to sweet music and watch the best *hula* dancers of Moloka'i, for I am high chief of that island and I shall make you my chiefess."

"No! No! No!" Hina cried. "There is a mistake. I am married already. My husband is the chief of Hilo and I have sons, eleven—no, twelve—fine sons. I cannot marry you."

The high chief laughed softly as the canoe flew over the waves toward Moloka'i.

❦ ❦ ❦

Meanwhile Hina's serving women searched for her. Soon word was carried to the chief. The houses of Hilo were searched and fishermen paddled over the bay stopping at every rock and sand bar, for no one had seen the strange canoe.

The chief's sons joined the search, all but Nīheu. His father found his eleventh son sitting sadly by a fire. He stirred the fire with a stick and looked into the flames as if they pictured trouble. "Up!" his father shouted. "Up, and search for your mother!"

Nīheu made a sign for "No." He was still looking into the fire and spoke slowly as if reading the message of the flames. "It is no use," he said. "Hina has been stolen by the high chief of Moloka'i. He has carried her to Hā'upu Hill where he would make her his wife."

"He cannot!" the chief shouted. "She is my wife!"

Nīheu still looked sadly into the flames. "That is what she tells him," he answered. "She will not marry him and he says that he will keep her prisoner on Hā'upu Hill and you shall never have her back."

"We will go to Moloka'i and fight!" the chief cried.

"We cannot," the young man answered. "The high chief of Moloka'i has a mighty army. More than that, Hā'upu Hill is a place our army can never take."

"Then we shall go by night," the chief said. "You and your brothers shall climb Hā'upu Hill and steal away your mother in the darkness."

Again Nīheu made a sign for "No," as he sadly watched the flames. "None of us can do this," he replied. "In the fire I see that hill of Hā'upu. I see that some power lifts it up and up, until no man can reach its top."

"What power, my son?"

Nīheu looked long into the flames. "I do not know," he said at last. "Something holds Hā'upu Hill and lifts it. I cannot see what power it is."

❦ ❦ ❦

Kana, in his upland home, knew nothing of what had happened to his mother. He was a man now, doing all the heavy work for his grandmother and seemingly content. But old Uli knew he needed to use his strength and power in other ways. She knew of Hina's trouble and that Kana, only, could rescue her. But Uli waited.

One day, as the two worked together in the garden, Kana lifted his head to listen. "Uli," he said, "what is the sound I hear?" The old woman did not answer. Hardly knowing what he did, Kana dropped his digging stick and started down the trail, drawn by the sound. Old Uli watched him go. The time had come!

The trail led to the village. There Kana found a crowd of men and boys. It was their shouting that he had heard, faintly, in the upland. "What is going on?" Kana asked someone.

"See that huge fish!" The man pointed. "The sons of the chief are trying to lift it. It is very heavy and slippery but Nīheu, the youngest, can lift and carry it. He has great strength."

"The others must be weak," said Kana.

The man laughed. "*Ē!* You chiefs!" he shouted. "Here is a country boy who calls you weak ones!"

The chief's sons turned angrily toward the stranger. A boy from the country with the mud of a garden upon him! Did he dare to call them weak ones? "Let us see you lift the fish!" they said.

Kana waded eagerly into the bay. He caught the fins of the great fish and struggled to get a firm hold. He had never before tried to lift a fish and, for a moment, did not know what to do with the slippery flopping thing. At last he held it firmly, threw it on his back, waded to shore and started up the trail. "This will make a fine gift for Grandmother," he was thinking.

The chief's sons were angry to see this country fellow walk easily away with their fish. "Thief!" they shouted, and ran after him.

They caught Kana and tied him to a tree. The ten brothers carried their fish back to Hilo but Nīheu stayed to watch the prisoner. He wondered about this strong boy from the upland. He is even stronger than I, the young man thought. He walked off with that fish as if it had no weight at all!

Someone was coming down the path. It was old Uli, the wise one, his grandmother. "*Aloha,* Grandmother!" Nīheu said. "Here is a thief from the upland. He was trying to steal our fish. Do you know him?"

"He is no thief," Uli replied. "This is Kana, your young brother. He is the strongest and wisest of you all. Come, Kana!" she called.

At her word the boy shook off the ropes that bound him. He shook them off as if they had been no more than threads spun by a spider. Then he followed the old woman up the trail.

A long time Nīheu stood looking after them. This was his brother, this boy with strength and wisdom! He too is a son of Hina! the young man said to himself. He can rescue her.

Nīheu went into the forest where he worked for days. At last he went in search of Kana. "You are my brother," he said. "Hina, our mother, is a prisoner on Hāʻupu Hill. You are the one who can rescue her. I have built a canoe in the forest. Help me launch it. Then go with me to Molokaʻi to steal away our mother."

"I will go," Kana replied.

Nīheu led his brother into the forest and showed him the canoe. "Go down to the launching place," said Kana. "I shall push the canoe down to you. Be ready to leap into it."

Nīheu looked at Kana in great surprise. He looked long. Then he turned and hurried down the mountainside to the launching place.

He had hardly reached the bay when he saw the canoe shoot down the mountain toward him. It shot down swiftly as a sled slipping over a grassy slide. The young man had only time to spring into the canoe as it slid past and he was carried out into the bay.

Kana waded to him, bringing paddles. "You shall paddle to Molokaʻi," Kana said. "I shall wrap myself in *kapa* and lie hidden in the bottom of the canoe. The plan is yours. You, alone, shall rescue our mother."

The older brother hesitated. "I will try," he said, "but I do not think that I can do this thing."

"If you need me, I am ready," Kana answered.

His *kahuna* came to the high chief of Molokaʻi. "Last night I dreamed, O Heavenly One," he said. "Set free this woman you hold prisoner. If you do not, you and all your people will be destroyed."

"Not so!" The high chief laughed. "No one can conquer Hā‘upu Hill. I shall keep this woman until she is willing to be my wife. She is as beautiful as the rising sun and her hair is as soft and shining as the feathers of the ‘ō‘ō bird."

The *kahuna* spoke again. "O Heavenly One," he said, "send for another *kahuna*. Do not let this evil find you unprepared."

"Very well," the high chief answered, "but I do not fear the words of four hundred of you!"

Another *kahuna* came, a woman. She filled a great wooden bowl with water and covered it with *kapa*. She prayed and waited. At last she lifted the *kapa* and the two looked. The woman turned to the high chief. "I see him here," she said. "I see a man so tall that he can reach the top of Hā‘upu Hill. He will take the prisoner and destroy you and all your people."

"I fear him not!" shouted the chief. "Let him stretch to his full height. Hā‘upu Hill rests on the back of a great turtle. At my command the turtle can lift it up and up till no man can reach its top. Go! I do not fear your words! Hina shall be my wife."

The two turned to go. They looked over the sea and cried, "A strange canoe! Even now danger comes."

The chief looked. One canoe was coming, paddled by one small man! The chief heard his men calling, "Is that a war canoe or are you a traveler?"

"A war canoe!" the small man shouted bravely.

The high chief laughed. "Guard the prisoner well," he commanded. "This one may try to steal the woman away by night."

That was what Nīheu tried to do. In the darkness he climbed the cliff where no guard thought of danger.

No man saw or heard him.

But one of the chief's birds heard the slipping of a stone. In the darkness the form of a man! The little bird

flew at the dark form. Startled, the young man struck at the bird, lost his hold, slipped and fell. Sadly he returned to the canoe. "I knew I could not do it," he told Kana.

Now the guards of the high chief were ready. As Kana stretched to his full height they saw his form against the starlit sky. "Danger, O Heavenly One!" they shouted to the chief. "A tall one comes! He towers over Hā'upu Hill!"

"Show your strength, my turtle!" the chief commanded. "Lift up the hill."

Up and up rose Hā'upu Hill. Kana watched it. How could it grow so high? What power lifted it? The top was far above his head. "I too have failed!" thought the young man sadly.

Then he seemed to hear the voice of Uli. "The turtle, O Kana!" The words came faintly to his ears as in a dream, but the voice was his grandmother's. "The great turtle of the chief holds Hā'upu on its back and lifts it. Break its flippers, O my grandson!"

Using all his mighty strength Kana broke the flippers of the giant turtle, first those on the left, then those on the right. The power of the turtle was destroyed. It sank down and with it sank the hill which crumbled and fell with a crash. Trees, houses and people were swallowed in a mighty opening of the earth. Only the two *kāhuna*, the man and the woman, were ready for the crash. They alone were saved—these two and Hina, for Kana had seized his mother in his arms as the hill sank.

Gently he laid her in the canoe and he and Nīheu started back to Hilo. Hina watched the strong arms which sent the canoe through the waves as a bird flies through the air. She felt the freedom and joy of a bird. "It is because of Kana!" she thought and remembered the words of Uli, "The time will come when Kana, only, can rescue you." Those words were true.

From Hawaiian Legends *by Rice, used by permission of Bishop Museum Press, Bernice Pauahi Bishop Museum.*

How ʻUmi Became High Chief

Before Līloa, high chief of Hawaiʻi, died he called his sons to him in the presence of lesser chiefs and his wise *kahuna.* "Hākau, my older son, shall be high chief," he said, "and ʻUmi, his young brother, shall be his man. ʻUmi, give loyal service to your chief. Hākau, respect your man." Did Līloa hope that his dying words would change the nature of his older son?

For Hākau had been a jealous boy. He had never liked his handsome popular young brother. He was jealous of ʻUmi's strength and skill, jealous of his three loyal companions and jealous of the praise that he often overheard. In sports ʻUmi and his companions were often victors over Hākau and his friends. Hākau's jealousy showed itself in scornful words and in small unkind acts.

And his nature did not change. He proved a jealous cruel chief. If he heard praise of one of his lesser chiefs he watched for a chance to do that one some harm. He took from others things that he liked: a beautiful *kapa,* a fine weapon or a child to be his servant. So Hākau came to have enemies among the chiefs and the fear and hatred of the common people.

As for ʻUmi, he tried to obey his father's last command. For some time he gave loyal service to his brother but, as Hākau's unkind treatment became open cruelty, ʻUmi grew very angry. One day he took his three companions aside. "Waipiʻo is not big enough for both Hākau and me," he said. "He is the chief. Let us go away."

The three friends hated Hākau and were glad to go. The four slipped away by night and journeyed toward the east. By the time they reached the Hilo district they had a plan. "Let us live among the people as common men," said 'Umi. "People will take us in and give us food in return for our work. We can take new names and no one will recognize us."

"But it is not right that you work among common men, 'Umi," his friends objected. "We shall work but you cannot, for you are a chief." 'Umi agreed. There would be time for surfing and other sports he loved.

The four entered a village and made friends with the people. 'Umi said his name was Hānai and gave the new names of his friends. The people of the village liked the looks of these young men, especially Hānai. His muscles were well developed. He looked as if he could work! And he was eagerly invited to many homes. When Hānai had chosen one, his friends were invited. The farmer whose home Hānai had chosen was very proud. But he soon found the young man was no worker!

In wrestling, boxing or surfing Hānai was always first and was admired and praised. But when it came to fishing and farming, he did no work and brought home no food. The man in whose home Hānai stayed was not pleased. "Oh, he can roll a *maika* stone," this man said to a friend, "but if he would use his arms in paddling a fishing canoe—that is what this family needs!" Hānai did not hear these words but he saw black looks.

One day the canoes were going *aku* fishing. When someone called to him, "Come and paddle," Hānai went gladly, for *aku* fishing was a sport he loved. When the canoes returned he was given a fish and climbed the cliff to offer it before a little image of Kū'ula, the fish god. He did not know that a rainbow hung over him as he climbed. But a certain wise *kahuna* saw and wondered.

A rumor came that 'Umi, the young chief, had disappeared from Waipi'o. "And I have seen a rainbow over this stranger as he climbed the cliff," the *kahuna* thought. He took a small black pig and went to Hānai.

"What have you there?" Hānai asked.

"An offering," the *kahuna* told him. "This is a chief-searching pig." He put the little pig on the ground and it ran straight to Hānai. "Tell me," said the *kahuna,* "are you 'Umi?"

"Yes, I am 'Umi," the young man answered.

"Then come and live with me," the *kahuna* said. In his own mind he added, "Hākau is a cruel chief. This boy will be a greater man than the older brother. I shall care for him and train him and I shall watch for the chance to make 'Umi high chief of Hawai'i."

One day the *kahuna* told 'Umi of a message he had received. "Two old men are coming," he said, "two wise old men whom your father loved. They were his advisors. He gave them food and all things that they needed. But Hākau does not like those who give good advice. He shows no kindness to the old men. So they have left Waipi'o and are coming here. I think they are coming to see what sort of man you have become. They are important men and I want them to notice you and think well of you. This is my plan. Tomorrow I shall take my servants and go to the fields to work, leaving you at home to greet the old men and give them food."

'Umi lifted his head proudly. Preparing food and heating an *imu* were not the work of chiefs! He had never done such work. Still he said nothing but listened to the plan. He smiled when he had heard it. Yes, he could do what was needed.

The *kahuna* chopped a log then tied it up so that it looked like an uncut log. He caught a little pig and tied it not far from the house. He prepared food for cooking, heated the *imu* and prepared *'awa.* Then he dug up an *'awa* bush and put it back into the ground covering the roots so that it seemed to be growing.

Early in the morning he went to the fields to work followed by all his servants. 'Umi alone was left at home. Soon two old men appeared and 'Umi made them welcome. "The *kahuna* has gone to the fields with his men," he told them. "Only I am left but I shall prepare food. Sit in the shade and rest."

As they rested the two watched the young man, thinking he was a servant of the *kahuna*. They saw him split a large log with one blow of his stone adze. Soon a fire was blazing. Leaves thrown on the burning wood made a thick smoke so that the old men could no longer watch 'Umi. But they heard sounds as if he prepared an *imu*. They heard the grunt of a pig and thought he was killing it to cook. They were very hungry and it was hard to wait until the food should be ready.

They watched the young man go off a little distance and pull up an *'awa* bush. Such strength! He had it up with a single pull! They saw him bringing an *'awa* bowl and water. Then the smoke hid him but they thought he was preparing *'awa*.

In a very short time 'Umi set food before the old men—pork, potatoes and other food they loved. "Never have we had such food since Hākau became chief," they said to each other, "and so quickly cooked! Never in our lives have we seen any man who could prepare an *imu* and so quickly serve the food. Surely this servant has power from the gods!"

Then 'Umi brought the *'awa*. Only a few moments ago they had seen him pull up an *'awa* bush and now the *'awa* drink was ready! Wonderful!

"Eat, drink and rest," 'Umi said to the old men. "I shall go up to the fields to tell the *kahuna* you are here."

Soon the *kahuna* returned and welcomed his guests. "Have you all the things you need?" he asked them.

"We have both food and drink," they answered. "The young man who was here served us as we never have been served in all our lives. Where is he?"

"My men will come from the fields at nightfall," the *kahuna* said.

Then the three talked together. They talked of Hākau's cruelty. "The people fear and hate him," the old men said. "Hawai'i needs a better chief."

They asked about 'Umi and the *kahuna* said, "I have great love for him. He is both wise and strong. He will be a greater man than Hākau."

"Where is the young chief?" one asked.

The *kahuna* did not answer but turned to watch his servants who were coming down the trail carrying their digging sticks. The old men also watched. One man came a little behind the others. Mist was falling and in the light of the full moon the old men saw a rainbow over this last man. "The young chief!" they whispered. Then, as he passed them, they knew him for the one who had prepared their food and drink.

"He served us, our chief?" said one. "It was not right that a son of Līloa should act as a servant."

"But such a servant!" the other answered. "He surely has power from the gods. Let 'Umi rule Hawai'i."

The *kahuna* was pleased. With the help of these two 'Umi could indeed become high chief. The *kahuna* had faith that the young man would become a wise and strong chief. He was pleased with the success of his plan.

The advice and influence of the old men was enough. Hākau was overthrown and 'Umi became chief. The *kahuna* led him to the *heiau*. There he spoke solemnly:

> "Listen, O Heavenly One!
> The gods have helped you
> To overcome poverty

And to become the great chief of Hawai'i.
Rule wisely and you shall rule long.
Give ear to these words and live."

Then the *kahuna* gave a spear to one of 'Umi's companions. "It is a sacred spear," he said, "a testing spear. Hurl it at 'Umi. Hurl it with all your strength." Spear in hand, the young man took his place. 'Umi watched as his friend balanced the spear for a moment, aimed it and then hurled it with all his strength. 'Umi caught the spear with his right hand and held it. The *kahuna* was pleased.

"O 'Umi," he said,
"As you caught this spear and held it firmly
So shall you hold Hawai'i and rule firmly."

His words proved true. 'Umi became a great high chief. He ruled Hawai'i firmly and made wise laws for the people. Because he had lived for a time among fishermen and farmers 'Umi understood their work. He had great *kalo* patches made in Waipi'o. He taught his servants and even worked among them in the fields. He took his place among the *aku* fishers.

🐚 🐚 🐚

One day the *kahuna* said, "O Heavenly One, the time has come for you to marry. Take for your wife Pi'ikea, young chiefess of Maui. In that way lasting peace will be made between these two islands."

'Umi respected the *kahuna* as a father and listened to his words. "It is well," he said and chose one of his companions to go to the father of Pi'ikea.

'Umi's friend found great excitement on the landing beach when he reached Maui. He heard shouts and saw people running about in great confusion. "Is it war or peace?" a guard called to him.

"Peace!" answered ‘Umi's friend. These people had feared an attack from Hawai‘i! They would be glad to arrange this marriage.

He was taken before the high chief. "Why do you come?" he was asked, and ‘Umi's friend understood that the chief, also, feared war with ‘Umi's men.

"O Heavenly One, may you live long," said the young man from Hawai‘i. "‘Umi, our chief, wishes your daughter for his wife. He wishes peace between Maui and Hawai‘i."

The chief of Maui was pleased. "These are good words," he said. Soon shouting was heard outside. The people rejoiced for it was a great honor that their young chiefess should be the wife of mighty ‘Umi. This marriage would mean years of peace.

After days of games and feasting ‘Umi's friend made ready to return. Then Pi‘ikea came to him.

> "You return to Hawai‘i," she said.
> "Take my *aloha* to ‘Umi, your great chief.
> Tell him Pi‘ikea is glad to become his wife.
> Tell him I think of him both day and night.
> Even in sleep I dream of him.
> In twenty days I shall reach Waipi‘o.
> May his life be long and may he rule wisely."

‘Umi listened to this message brought by his friend. Then he asked, "Is she good to look at, this Pi‘ikea?"

"She is very beautiful, O Heavenly One. There is no woman in Hawai‘i like this young girl. From the top of her head to the soles of her feet she is perfect in every way."

‘Umi was pleased. Peace with Maui was good and a beautiful wife would be good also. "Make ready for the coming of the young chiefess," he commanded.

Twenty days later the channel between Maui and Hawai‘i was filled with canoes. Every person who lived in

Waipi'o was on the beach watching. "That is her canoe," 'Umi exclaimed, "for its sail is red."

Everyone watched eagerly. As the canoes came near the one with the red sail took the lead. Now people could see that this canoe was altogether red. Each paddler wore a red *malo* and even the paddles were red. 'Umi's eyes were on the beautiful young girl who looked eagerly toward her new home.

Rain clouds had gathered. As the red canoe came close, a light rain fell. Thunder roared and suddenly a small rainbow appeared just above the canoe of the young chiefess. It arched from end to end of the canoe like the arching top of a huge helmet. "The gods are pleased," said the *kahuna*.

'Umi and Pi'ikea were married and lived long in peace and happiness.

From Hawaiian Antiquities and Folklore *by Fornander.*

The Giant Guard

The sound of wailing rose on the night air and echoed from the cliffs of Waipi'o. In his sleeping house 'Umi listened, then called a servant. "That is my wife's voice," he said. "Why is Pi'ikea wailing?"

"Her brother has come," the servant answered, "Kiha, her young brother."

"He must be made welcome!" 'Umi exclaimed. "See that a feast is prepared."

The chief did not go at once to greet his brother-in-law, thinking the sister and brother would want a little time together. But he listened to his wife's voice. For a few moments the wailing stopped as if the two talked quietly. Then it rose again, more loud and shrill than before. Something is wrong, thought 'Umi and went to his wife.

In the torchlight her face was pale and streaked with tears. The usually quiet gentle girl seemed beside herself with grief. "O Pi'ikea, why do you weep?" her husband asked.

"For my brother," she answered, leading him forward. "This is Kiha, my young brother. It is long since I have seen him—long, long since we surfed together or slid together over waterfalls. Talk of those old days has brought tears to my eyes."

"That is the wailing of joy," said 'Umi, holding her in his arms. "Did I not hear, also, the wailing of sorrow?"

"That was for the cruelty my brother has borne. Always our older brother was jealous and unkind. We had little love for him. Now he is chief and openly cruel to Kiha. Oh, he has done to my brother things that cannot be borne!" She began to weep again. "It has come to war between them. But what can Kiha do with his few followers?

We must help him, 'Umi. We must go with many fighting men, conquer Maui, and make Kiha its high chief."

"No, Pi'ikea," said 'Umi gently. "When I married you I promised peace with Maui. I cannot break that promise."

"You promised my father," Pi'ikea answered, looking earnestly into her husband's face. "He is dead. Your promise to him does not prevent your aiding his good son against the evil one."

Still 'Umi hesitated. His blood tingled at the thought of war—its excitement and gain, but there was another side. This would mean taking men from their farms and their fishing. It might mean the loss of many men, and for what end? To make Kiha high chief of Maui. What good or gain would come to 'Umi and Hawai'i? He hesitated.

Pi'ikea drew away from him. "Oh 'Umi," she said, "you do not love me! Pi'ikea has been a good wife, fulfilling your every wish. Now she asks one thing of you, help for her best-loved brother, and you refuse! Life is no longer good. Let Pi'ikea die!" Her wailing rose again, bitter with grief.

'Umi had great love for his wife. Her words and wailing conquered him. "Hush!" he whispered, "it shall be as you wish." Calling a servant he said, "Summon my *kahuna* and my three companions."

The *kahuna* came at once, the old man who had been a foster father to 'Umi and had made him high chief. "Tell me, my *kahuna*," 'Umi said, "shall we war with Maui to make this young man chief? And what will come of it? Defeat or victory?"

"Victory!" the *kahuna* said at once. "I have dreamed of this war. Go to Maui and win gloriously."

The three companions had come in and heard these words. Already their faces were alight with eagerness for war. "Go," 'Umi told them, "go throughout Hawai'i and bid all men make ready. Tell them to make canoes, to carve spears of hard wood and braid the slings for sling shots. Tell them to make ready for war with Maui." The three friends went at once, rejoicing in the thought of war.

The making of canoes and weapons took much time but at last warriors came to Waipi'o. They came in canoes from all parts of the island until the beaches were covered with more men than 'Umi could count. All were filled with excitement of war and longing for conquest. 'Umi too, splendid in feather cape and helmet, was tingling with eagerness to fight.

Warriors with women and children loaded the canoes. The channel between the islands was filled with them. Sunlight gleamed on the red and gold of feather capes, on the image of the war god, on polished wood of weapons and strong bodies of fighting men. When the first canoes paddled into the bay of Hāna the last were just leaving Waipi'o Beach.

No wonder the hearts of the people of Hāna were filled with fear! But Hāna had Ka'uiki Hill. Men, women, children and animals withdrew to that hill. As 'Umi looked at Ka'uiki's cliffs he knew victory would not be easy.

"We can attack from the back," the three companions said, and 'Umi appointed the first to take men and reconnoiter. After a time the party returned. "A slope leads to Ka'uiki from the back," the young chief said. "From that slope rises the cliff, high and steep as you see in front. Men reach it by a ladder. Above that ladder rocks are poised ready to fall upon an enemy. Warriors wait with stones. An attack by day cannot be made. Tonight we shall try."

The men were eager for the night attack and stole away through the darkness. "The Maui men feel safe upon their hill," they thought. "Their guard will not be strong. We shall climb silently, take them by surprise and conquer them."

Soon they were back and, in the torchlight, 'Umi saw their eyes big with wonder and fear. "There is a guard," the young chief said, while his men gestured with their arms to show the size. "He is such as none of us has ever seen. Largest of the large, he is, and tallest of the tall! A giant, he stands at the ladder's top with a huge club ready to strike us, man by man, as we climb up. We cannot take that hill!"

'Umi saw these men were ready to return at once to their own island. Their fear might spread among the others. "Wait," he said. "Tomorrow we may have another plan."

Next day the second companion reconnoitered. He saw the ladder and men ready with rocks. "But no tall guard," he said. "We shall attack tonight." His men were making fun of those who went the night before. "Those men dreamed a giant guard!" they laughed. "In the dark a man looked like a giant!"

A few hours later their eyes were large with fear. "We saw him plainly," they were whispering. "Such a man we never saw since we were born! There he stands against the starlit sky, a giant indeed, with a club which would surely end us, one by one, as we stepped off the ladder. We saw him very plainly: his huge shoulders, his firm-wrapped *malo,* and that club made from the trunk of a great tree. Attack is hopeless!" Fear spread through the camp.

"Tomorrow I shall go!" said Pi'imai, the third of 'Umi's friends. "Tomorrow I shall face these dangers. Who will go with me?"

His courage chased away the fear and many arms were raised. "Let me go, O Pi'imai!" came from many throats.

Next day they went. From the bottom of the hill they saw the ladder. They saw great rocks poised at the cliff top and many warriors ready. "Wait here!" Pi'imai commanded. "Let us see what they will do."

Alone he climbed the hill. His men watched, breathless, as a rain of stones fell around him. Pi'imai whirled his club. As a man could ward off many spears with one, so Pi'imai with that whirling club struck aside every stone. He reached the ladder's foot and stood there whirling his war club. At last they saw him turn and come slowly down the hill still guarding himself with his stout club.

Out of range of the stones at last, he was welcomed by a mighty shout. "Such courage!" said his men. "Such skill! 'Umi must know."

"Climb by day, we cannot," Pi'imai told his chief. "But I saw nothing of that giant guard."

"By day he sleeps," said the warriors who had seen the giant.

"It may be," Pi'imai answered. "Tonight my men and I shall see."

They saw him in the starlight—a huge figure black against the sky. Pi'imai watched him as he and his men climbed the hill. "He stands very still," the young chief said. "I will challenge him and see what he will do. Stand back. No need for all to die."

Then Pi'imai moved closer and twirled his club in challenge. He waited. The giant did not move. Perhaps he cannot see me, the young chief thought and started up the ladder. Now! he told himself, I see that giant plainly. He must see me! Pi'imai twirled his club again. No answer.

Did this great man not know the meaning of the twirling club? He is not skilled in a war club's use, the young chief thought. Tense with excitement, yet curious and fearless, he climbed on. Again he twirled his club, first with right hand, then with left. No answer.

He reached the ladder's end. He was aware of the broad top of Ka'uiki and of many sleeping men but his

eyes were on the giant guard who loomed huge against the sky, yet without movement. Pi'imai twirled his club once more. The guard stood ready, club in hand, but made no answering move. Well, I'll strike you! the young man thought. I'll run in, strike and dodge your blow.

He darted close and gave the giant a warning tap. He heard a hollow sound as when a club hits wood! The giant did not move. Pi'imai went close and touched him. 'Ā! A wooden man! A wooden man had filled the warriors of 'Umi with great fear!

Pi'imai took the figure in his arms and threw it from the cliff. His men heard the wooden thing break as it fell. They, also, saw the trick and in a moment came swarming up the ladder.

Roused from sleep, the warriors of Maui found themselves already conquered. The chief was killed and Kiha made high chief. In gratitude he gave the district of Hāna to 'Umi. That is the way in which Hāna, on Maui, came to belong to Hawai'i.

From Hawaiian Antiquities and Folklore *by Fornander.*

The Wonderful Banana Skin

"**M**y son, I know you long for travel. You long to see Far Kahiki, those islands of which we hear strange tales. Yet you have stayed with me. You have stayed to care for an old man and lay his bones to rest in a secret cave. My life is finished and my bones shall rest here in Kalapana, the land I love. It is well.

"To you, my son, I have given all my wisdom. You know the prayers, the strong prayers, that call upon the gods. I have taught you prayers that will overcome all the evil you may meet. I have taught you the wisdom of canoe building. I have taught you to find stone for tools and weapons and to chip the stone. All my wisdom I have passed on to you.

"One last gift is left." The old man took from a fold of his *malo* a banana, yellow and ripe. "Keep this, my son," he said. "Eat when you are hungry, but save the skin. Never lose it nor let it be taken from you. May the gods care for you in your travels and bring you safe, at last, back to Kalapana."

The son, Kūkali, obeyed his father's words and laid the old man's bones to rest in a secret cave. Then he stood looking over the ocean. He was free! Free now to voyage to Far Kahiki, those islands of which other voyagers had told. Kūkali saw how the sky rests on the ocean all about Hawai'i. There he would sail, for Far Kahiki lay beyond. He must make ready for his journey.

Taking strong adzes, the young man followed the trail to the forest where stood tall *koa* trees. He prayed as his father had taught him, made offering and chose a tree. Then he rested and ate the banana his father had given him. It seemed strange to save the skin but those were his father's words and his father had been a wise *kahuna*. So Kūkali put the skin safely within his *malo* and set to work with his adze. He worked till darkness fell, then wrapped his *kapa* about him and lay down to sleep.

He awoke rested but hungry. He thought of the banana he had eaten. Perhaps a little of the fruit was left. He took it from his *malo*—a whole banana! So this was the secret of his father's parting gift, a banana skin that would be ever full of food. A good gift indeed! Kūkali ate and went to work.

Many days he worked in the forest, cutting down the *koa* tree, cutting off branches and fashioning a canoe. Day after day he ate his banana, always ripe and nourishing. And day after day he dreamed of the voyage he would make.

At last he dragged the small canoe to the sea, finished and then launched it. He took nothing with him but his banana skin and the wisdom of his father. He prayed to the gods of the winds. He steered by the sun by day and the stars by night and came, at last, to one of the islands of Far Kahiki.

Kūkali was very tired with days and nights of sailing. When he had beached his canoe he threw himself on the dry sand and slept. His sleep was heavy. Strange dreams came, wind blew and Kūkali shivered with cold and fear but for many hours he did not waken.

When at last he woke, the young man was surprised to see a crowd of people watching him. They were thin, pale people who seemed ready for death.

"Who are you?" Kūkali asked, sitting up. He looked about him. He was no longer on the beach but in a deep, dark valley whose cliff walls shut out the sun. "Where am I?"

"In the valley of the giant bird," a man replied and his voice was full of sadness. "While you slept that great bird found you and brought you here, as he brought all of us."

"Yes," said another voice, "and there is no way to escape from this valley. Here we die."

"There is no food," said a third man hopelessly. "We die of hunger."

Hunger! Kūkali sprang to his feet and drew forth the banana. "Here is food!" he cried.

The people crowded close and looked at the banana, wild with longing. "It is so small," one said. "Let us divide it and each one have a taste."

"No," Kūkali answered, "you eat it all. You shall see. All of you shall be fed."

The man ate while others watched hungrily. When he had finished Kūkali held out his hand for the skin. "Now you," he said, turning to the next man. The skin was again filled with ripe fruit. Kūkali saw hope light the faces of the crowd. By nightfall all were fed.

"Tell me about the giant bird," Kūkali said.

"He rules this island," one answered. "He brings all its people to this valley from which there is no escape. He has brought all who live upon the island and also every voyager who has landed here. All day he flies about searching for victims or lights upon the cliff to see how many of us have died of hunger."

"No more shall die of hunger," Kūkali said. "Now let us plan."

During the days that followed all the people of the valley were fed with the wonderful banana. Soon they were strong enough to work and there was work for them. Kūkali found hard rock like that which came from Mauna Kea. He taught the men to chip it and taught them prayers. He showed them how to make handles of wood and tie these firmly to the sharpened stone. "We must have weapons," he said. "Some day we shall be ready to fight the giant bird." And Kūkali prayed. He prayed for victory and freedom. He knew the gods would help, for these were prayers his father had taught him. These prayers would overcome all evil.

Every day the bird came to look for dead. The people knew when he was coming for they felt the wind of his wings before they saw the bird. There was time to hide among the rocks. Sometimes the bird lighted on the cliff top and looked long into the valley, cocking his head this way and that. "He is searching for the dead," whispered a man hiding beside Kūkali. "Since you came with food there are no dead. The giant bird is wondering."

At last weapons were ready. Plans were made, the final prayers were said and the people were full of courage. "The wind!" someone shouted. "The giant bird is coming!"

While some hid, weapons in hand, a few dropped to the floor of the valley and lay still as if in death. The bird flew down. Suddenly the dead men rose and struck while from every side others attacked. The battle was fought up and down the valley floor—a fierce battle. Badly hurt, the great bird tried to fly away but men held him by the wings and struck him again and again till he was dead.

Some men had deep wounds but not one had been killed. Even the wounded worked now with great hope. Some gathered wood to pile about the bird and kindled a huge fire. In that fire the body of the giant bird was destroyed.

Others were cutting footholds in the cliff wall. When these were ready Kūkali prayed once more. He felt the power of the gods and climbed. Holding strong vines he cut more footholds. Up and up he climbed. At last the cliff top was reached. Sunshine! Safety! Once again he saw the blue ocean beyond which lay Hawai'i!

Kūkali turned to help the others. One by one they climbed, the strong helping the weaker ones. The last one reached the cliff top. For a moment they looked back into the dark valley. Only a thin line of smoke showed where the giant bird had been slain.

Men turned their eyes to their broken houses and deserted farms. "Come with us, Kūkali," they said. "You have saved us. Our gardens are full of food. We shall rebuild our houses and dig in the good earth or sail the sea. Come with us, Kūkali, and make this land your home."

Kūkali looked where his own canoe still waited on the beach. "No, friends," he said, "I thank you for the offer. My *aloha* to you but I sail back to Kalapana. Hawai'i is my home."

From Legends of Gods and Ghosts *by Westervelt.*

The Boy Who Came To His Father

"Who is my father?" Nī'au had asked that question when he was a tiny boy.

"You have no father," Hina said. "There is just you and me—no more."

When he got older Nī'au asked again. "Other boys have fathers," he said. "Who is my father?"

"You have no father," his mother answered as before. "There is just you and me—no more." The boy wondered. Again and again he asked.

Now he had grown to manhood. "Mother," he said, "you cannot put me off. Tell me the truth. Who is my father? Is he dead? Did he leave us? I must know."

Then Hina led him to a cave. "Here are your father's tokens," she said.

Nī'au pushed away vines and bushes. Under a ledge of rock he found a canoe and turned to his mother. "This?" he asked.

"Yes. This and more."

In the canoe the boy found mast and sail. A red sail? Red is the color of a chief. He found a feather cape and helmet of royal red. He turned to his mother, his eyes dark with wonder. "The tokens of a chief!" he cried. "My father is a chief! Where is he? Where does he live?"

Hina beckoned him to sit beside her on a rock. She told him how, years ago, she had found a stranger lying in the edge of the waves. "I thought at first that he was dead, but he was not. I pulled him out of reach of the waves and ran for my father who gave the stranger drink and food and led him to our house.

"Soon he was strong and well again. He stayed with us and he and I were married. He never told me where he had come from. At first I wondered. Then I was happy to have him and did not think about the past. I was happy to have him help my father with the fishing and farming, happy to hear him sing, or to surf with him. I forgot to wonder about the days that were past or the days that were to come.

"Then one day he said, 'I must leave you.'

"I was frightened. 'Where are you going?' I asked. 'Will you soon come back?'

"His face was sad. 'My father is a chief in Far Kahiki,' he told me. 'Last night he came to me in a dream. "My son," he said, "I am growing old. I need you." I must obey my father's call.'

"'But you will come back?' I asked again.

"'I cannot return,' he answered. 'In time I shall be chief and a chief has many duties. O Hina, when our son is born name him Nī'au. He shall be all yours until he is a man. Then give him my tokens hidden in the cave. Tell him his father waits for him. He shall wear my cape and helmet and come in my canoe. So I shall know my son.' Then your father left me.

"Now you are a man, Nī'au. The time has come for you to take the tokens and go to find your father."

The young man stood looking out over the ocean. "Far Kahiki!" he said softly. "My father is a chief in that far land and some day I shall be a chief. O Hina, I must go to my father. I must go now!"

"Yes, Nī'au," she said sadly. "You must go. Ask your grandfather for food and for his guiding arrow which will lead you. Launch your canoe, set your red sail—"

"No, no, Hina!" the young man said impatiently. "I cannot sail to Far Kahiki. That would take many days and I must go now! Now!"

Hina bowed her head sadly. "Tonight I shall talk with your grandfather," she replied.

Hina was awake at dawn. She stood before her house and prayed. She chanted a prayer to the guardian of her family, the Life-giving Coconut:

"O Life-giving Coconut,
That budded in Kahiki,
That rooted in Kahiki,
That formed a trunk in Kahiki,
That bore leaves in Kahiki,
That bore fruit in Kahiki,
That ripened in Kahiki,
Take this son of mine,
Take him to Kahiki."

So Hina prayed, then knelt upon the sand to watch a tiny plant.

The sky became pink, the ocean was like a great pink shell, even the sand was rosy. And in the rosy light the tiny plant became a tree—a strong young coconut tree. Already it bore two nuts.

Then Hina awakened her son. "The time has come," she said. She gave him a bundle wrapped in *kapa,* the cape and helmet.

"No," Nī'au told her, "I leave my father's things with you."

"But these are the tokens, my son. How else will your father know you?"

"A man will know his own son," Ni'au answered. "I cannot be burdened with the tokens."

Hina said, "Our guardian is ready and will take you in his arms." She led the boy to the coconut tree. "Climb," she said. "It is our guardian. But first take this bow and arrow, your grandfather's gift, to guide you. Climb the tree and hold it tight. You will be safe, Nī'au."

For a moment the young man held his mother close. Then he sprang into the tree, climbed and sat among the leaves. He waved his bow and shouted, "I go to Far Kahiki!"

The coconut tree shot up. Taller and taller it grew until Nī'au was only a speck. Then Hina heard him call: "O Hina! Hina! My hands and feet are numb with fear!"

Hina prayed, "O Life-giving Coconut, hold your grandchild fast," and Nī'au's fear was gone.

Taller and taller grew the tree until it seemed to reach to the deep blue of heaven. Hina could no longer see her son but she heard his voice, "O Hina! Hina! My hands and feet are numb with fear!"

Again she prayed, "O Life-giving Coconut, hold your grandchild fast." Once more Nī'au's fear was gone.

The tree bent over in a great arch. The top reached toward Kahiki. Down swung Nī'au and again he called, "O Hina! Hina! My hands and feet are numb with fear. I am losing my grip. I shall fall!"

Then Hina prayed with all her heart, "O Life-giving Coconut, take care of my son!"

The tree bent to the earth. Nī'au stepped off. He was in Kahiki. A tall man stood where the tree had been. "I am your guardian," he said. "Do not be afraid but shoot the guiding arrow. That will lead you." Suddenly the man was gone and Nī'au was alone.

He walked along the beach and heard the song of the waves. He looked at the mountains rising to the clouds.

This was Kahiki! Then he remembered the arrow and fitted it to his bow. "Lead me where I belong," he said and shot. He heard the whistling of the arrow and saw it fly. Over the beach! Over gardens! Into a house? Had it gone into that house? Nī'au was not sure.

He hurried after and reached the doorway of the house. "Have you seen my arrow?" he called.

"Your arrow?" answered a musical voice. Looking into the dark house he saw a girl. Her black hair hung about her and she wore a red *pā'ū* and many red *lehua lei*. She seemed to shine with beauty.

Nī'au stood looking at her. She was more beautiful than any girl in the world, he thought. She must be a young chiefess—but he was a young chief! "My arrow," he said. "I thought it came in here."

"Perhaps you were mistaken."

"May I call it?"

"Yes, call your arrow," the girl said, her face bright with laughter.

Nī'au called, "O arrow of my grandfather, where are you?"

"Here!" he heard the arrow answer.

"Come to me!" But the arrow did not come. Suddenly Nī'au knew. That beautiful laughing girl had caught his arrow and held it fast. This was where he belonged!

🐞 🐞 🐞

The husband of Hina had not forgotten. He was a busy chief, yet he thought of her in far Hawai'i and he thought of their son. A son? Yes, he was sure the child was a boy—Nī'au.

Sometimes he dreamed of the boy. He seemed to see him playing with little stones. Again he was catching crabs. Another time he was learning to swim. Years passed. The boy must have grown older. His grandfather must be teaching him to paddle a canoe and fish. At last he must be a man! The time had come! The chief seemed to see his son finding his canoe. He seemed to see his son pulling the *kapa* from the feather cape and helmet. Now Nī'au knew who his father was! He knew he was a young chief!

The father seemed to see his son leaving Hawai'i, sailing in the small canoe. The sail was red in the sunlight, the feather cape and helmet were bright red. Nī'au was on his way!

Then the father made ready for his son. He called his servants. "My son is coming," he said to them. "You must prepare for him. Prepare a house and all its furnishings and a swimming pool in the ocean's edge."

He set two guards to watch the sea. "Look for a small canoe," he commanded. "Soon you will see a canoe with a red sail. It is my son, your young chief. Run to me with the news." And he chose a wife for Nī'au. She was the daughter of a chief and she was beautiful and kind.

All things were ready. The chief looked at the swimming pool fed by sea waves and by a spring. Sunshine was on it and the shadow of a palm tree made it cool. Small bright fish played there. Nī'au would be happy in his pool.

The chief looked at the house. The pile of sleeping mats was thick and soft and the *kapa* soft and warm. A great wooden bowl held shoulder cape and *malo*. He lifted the cover and smelled the sweet smell of his son's clothes. He touched his son's drum and listened to its song. Soon Nī'au would be playing it!

The chief stood on the beach and looked. The ocean was blue and still. No red sail yet! But it would come! The watchers would run to tell him. He would welcome his son and hold him in his arms! He would lead him to his house. The girl would come and they would be married. They would love each other as he and Hina had loved.

"O Heavenly One, may you live long!" A servant had come running.

The chief forgot his dreams. "Do you bring news?" he asked.

"I bring news, O Heavenly One. The girl who was to marry your son—she has a husband! She has married a stranger! They—"

The angry words of the chief broke in. "Bad girl!" he shouted. "Bring her before me! Bring them both!"

The two were brought before the chief. He did not see the beauty of the girl or the fearless strength of the

young man. He did not see that this young man looked
like a chief. Angrily he spoke to the girl. "You had no
right to marry. You were to be the wife of my son. You
bad, bad girl."

The young chief answered fearlessly as he looked into
the chief's eyes. "I am your son," he said. "I am Nī'au."

"Then show me my canoe with its red sail! Show me
my cape and helmet!" The chief shouted in his anger.

"I left them with my mother in Hawai'i," the young
man answered.

"Liar!" the chief shouted. "You are not my son. You
have no red-sailed canoe. You have no cape and helmet.
Take him away!" he shouted to the servants. "Kill him!
Throw his body into the sea!"

The girl cried and clung to her husband. She tried to
speak but the chief would not listen. "Do as I command!"
he shouted. "Kill this man. Throw his body into the sea."
The servants did as their chief commanded but the Life-
giving Coconut kept Nī'au safe.

The chief's two guards still watched, both day and
night. They watched for a small canoe with a red sail. One
night they saw a young man come from the sea. He did
not come from a canoe but seemed to come out of the
sea itself. He stopped beside the new swimming pool and
looked at it. "O Kahikiloa! O Kahikipoko!" he called to
the guards. How did he know their names, they wondered. "Whose swimming pool is this?"

"It is Nī'au's," they answered.

The young man spoke in a low, sad voice. "They have
killed Nī'au," he said, "yet you say this is his swimming
pool." The stranger looked long at the pool. Then he
jumped in and swam.

He came out of the pool and stood before the house. "O Kahikiloa! O Kahikipoko!" he said. "Whose house is this?"

"It is Nī'au's," they answered.

"They have killed Nī'au," the stranger said again, "yet you say this house is his." He went in and they saw him drink from the water gourd. Who was this stranger? The men wondered and were afraid.

Soon he called to them, "O Kahikiloa! O Kahikipoko!" Whose drum is this?"

"It is Nī'au's."

"They have killed Nī'au, yet you say this drum is his," the young man said. He sat down and played upon the drum. He played long while the two men listened, wondered and were afraid.

At last he lay upon the bed of mats and pulled the *kapa* over him. He called softly, "O Kahikiloa! O Kahikipoko! Wake me early. I must go back before the sun is high." Then he slept.

When morning came the guards woke the young man. He sprang up, took a *malo* from the wooden bowl, put it on and ran swiftly down the beach. They saw him jump into the sea and swam away. Then he was gone as if the waves had swallowed him.

The next night the strange man came again out of the sea. He spoke to the two watchers as he had before. He swam, he played the drum and slept. In the morning he was gone into the sea.

So it was for four nights. Then the chief sent for his guards. "Kahikiloa, Kahikipoko," he said, "for four nights I have heard a drum. Its song is the song of my son's drum. Who has played upon it?"

"It was not a man who played," the guards replied. "It was a spirit who came up from the sea," and they told the chief what they had seen and heard.

The chief grew very sad. "It was my son," he whispered. "Nī'au came. The girl knew him but I did not. I
had him killed. Now his spirit comes each night. He
swims in my son's pool, he plays on my son's drum, he
sleeps on my son's mats. O my son! My son! I want you to
live! I want to hold you in my arms!"

He called his servants. "Make ready an offering," he
said. "Cook a black pig. Prepare black 'awa. Catch a red
and white fish."

All was done as the chief commanded. Then he
made offering to the Life-giving Coconut. "O Guardian
of my son," he prayed. "I have done wrong. I have killed
my own son. Forgive me. Show me how to make him
live again."

That night the chief and some of his men lay hidden
on the beach. They saw the young man rise from the sea.
He came out onto the beach and stood there in the
moonlight, tall and handsome. "O Kahikiloa! O
Kahikipoko!" he called. "I see eyes. Bright eyes are staring
at me from the sand."

The two guards answered, "There are crabs on the
beach. Sand crabs come out in the moonlight."

Then the young man went to the swimming pool.
"Whose pool is this?" he asked.

"It is Nī'au's," the guards replied.

"They have killed Nī'au," the young man said sadly,
"yet you say these things are his."

"Who are you?" asked the guards.

"I am Nī'au. My guardian, the Life-giving Coconut
brought me from Hawai'i. He bent over and bridged the
sea from Hawai'i to Kahiki. I found my wife. I came to find
my father but he would not listen. I had left the canoe
with its red sail, I had left the feather cape and helmet. I
had left these in Hawai'i with my mother and my father
did not know me. He had me killed." Then the young
man went into the house and lay upon the mats to sleep.

The chief had heard all this. The Life-giving Coconut had told him how to make Nīʻau live. Nets were wrapped about the house, an offering was made ready and Nīʻau's beautiful wife was brought.

The sun was high when the two guards woke the young man. He saw the sunlight and ran to the door, for Nīʻau's spirit wanted to escape into the sea. He felt himself caught in a net. He tore through it and tried to run, but another net held him. Suddenly he felt arms about him and looked into the face of his beautiful wife. He felt her love. She gave him food and he ate. Now he no longer wanted to dive into the sea, for he was a man as he had been before.

The chief had his son! The news was carried through the land. "The young chief has come home!" the people shouted. There was joy in Far Kahiki.

Told to Mary Kawena Pūkuʻi by her grandmother.

The Swing

"**O** Mother, do you hear that sound that comes faintly to us? It is not the sound of birds' wings in the air or of leaves shaken by the wind. What is it, O my mother?"

"It is the sound of shouting, Hiku, my son. Down by the beach many people are shouting."

"Why, Mother? Why do they shout?" the boy questioned eagerly.

"Perhaps young men are diving in an ocean pool. Perhaps they surf on the foaming waves. When one is very skillful others shout in praise."

"Diving?" asked Hiku thoughtfully. "Surfing? I want to do those things! O Mother, I long to go to the beach to learn to dive and surf! I want to hear the people shout when I do well!"

"No, Hiku! Your home is in the forest. Here there is sport enough. Climb the great trees, use arrow and spear and wrestle with wind and rain."

Hiku said no more but he did not forget. Diving and surfing! Someday I shall learn those sports, he told himself.

Years passed. Now and then the shouting at the beach came faintly to the boy and he would stop his work in the field or sport on the mountainside to listen and to wonder.

Sometimes he said to his mother, "When shall I learn the sports of the ocean?"

Always she put him off. "The sports of the forest and mountain are enough," or, "Wait till you become a man."

One day the shouting came to the mountain home more loud and clear. "Mother," said Hiku earnestly, "you can no longer put me off. I am a man. Today I go to learn to dive and surf."

The mother bent her head. "May the gods protect you from all evil," were her words as she watched her son rush down the mountainside.

Oh, the glory of that downward rush! Hiku scrambled over rocks, he clung to roots and vines, he met the rain and loved its fingers cooling him. Now and then he paused to listen. The shouting grew more clear. Then it stopped. He could hear nothing but the call of birds and rustle of the gentle wind.

He found a trail and came, at last, to an opening near the beach. Then he stopped to watch great waves roll, foaming, on the sand. And men, like himself, were riding the waves! How did they do it? Were they gods? He went on eagerly.

People were sitting about the beach, busy with games or talk. They looked up at the stranger, wondering.

"Why were you shouting?" Hiku asked.

"Our young chiefess was surfing," he was told. "Kāwelu rides the waves like a young goddess. The shouting was for her."

A chiefess! A young woman! Hiku thought. "Where is she now?" he asked.

"The morning's sport is over. She and her friends have gone to dress. The chiefess's home is over there." The people pointed and then watched Hiku as he hurried down the beach.

Hiku hurried and then slowed his steps. A chiefess! But I am a chief, he thought. Perhaps I can see this chiefess and talk with her.

At that moment a girl came from one of the houses. She wore a red *pā'ū* and many red *lehua lei*. Her damp hair hung about her. She came toward Hiku, saw him and stopped to look at the strange young man in wonder.

Hiku, too, had stopped. This girl was more lovely than the rosy clouds of dawn, more lovely than tiny birds flitting above blossoms. He had not known there was such beauty in the world! Admiration and great love woke in his heart and, as he looked, he saw love in the dark eyes of the girl.

Then she came to him. "You are welcome," she said softly. "Are you here to see our Kona Bay and its beaches? Then come. Men are diving and surfing still, though my friends and I were tired. Come and see them dive." She led him to an ocean pool. Hiku watched young men stand poised on the rocks, then leap, feet first, into the pool, curve through the water to the surface and swim back to climb and leap again.

For a time he watched and then, "I shall do that!" he said. He leaped into the water with a splash, came to the surface and swam to the rocks. He joined the laughter at his splashing. He watched and tried again.

"That was better!" the young chiefess said.

Once more Hiku tried, leaping into the water without a splash, curving to the surface and swimming quietly back to the rocks. "'Ā! Stranger! 'Ā!" He heard the shouts. He had dived well and people shouted for him!

"Come," he said. "Show me the surfing."

He watched the waves come dashing across the coral. He watched them break in foam and saw men ride them. They rode on long boards a little like the sled he used on grassy mountain slides. Oh, this was glorious sport! Laughter when a man fell with a splash and lost his sled! Shouts of praise when he rode safely to the beach! "I am going to surf," said Hiku to the chiefess.

She helped him choose his surf sled—a long smooth board, shaped and polished. He paddled out as he had seen the others do. The last line of breakers caught him, whirled him, snatched his board away and carried it high on the sand. There were shouts of laughter and Hiku joined them.

He got the board and paddled out again. He met breakers, ducked his head, hung on and found himself paddling toward larger breakers farther out. He slipped under his board as he had seen others do, clung to it as the water broke around him and paddled proudly toward the foaming line ahead. He watched great rollers coming, blue and green. There came the biggest of all! He paddled before it with all his strength.

The wave caught him. He was riding it! Perched on a rushing cliff he came shouting with joy and landed on the beach. All about him he heard shouts. "'Ā! The stranger! Child of the gods he must be! Who ever learned to ride the surf so quickly?"

The young chiefess's eyes were shining. "You are wonderful!" she said and then, "I am Kāwelu."

"And I, Hiku." He loved her and knew that she returned his love. She led him to her home and they became man and wife. The days that followed were glorious ones. Diving, surfing, playing on the beach! Resting together, watching the *hula* dancers or listening to a man who chanted tales of long ago! Each day some new sport or pleasure and always the companionship of the girl he loved!

Then, one morning as he woke, the thought of the forest came to Hiku. The cool touch of the mist, the chirp of waking birds—suddenly he longed for them! "Kāwelu," he whispered, "today I shall take you to the forest. I shall show you the beauty and sport of the upland. I shall teach you to ride my *hōlua*. I shall gather *lehua* blossoms and you will make us *lei*."

"No," answered the young chiefess and Hiku saw fear in her dark eyes. He said no more that day.

But the longing grew in him. He dreamed of mountain waterfalls, of the cold of mountain pools and of dangerous climbs over cliffside and rock. "Kāwelu," he said at last, "I must go back to the forest." Again he saw her fear. "You need not go," he added quickly. "Only let me leave you for a little while. Let me see my parents and grand-

father. Let me breathe cool air and drink cold water from
a mountain spring. Only a few days, Kāwelu!"

But she clung to him. "Do not leave me," she begged.
"Today there will be games—wrestling and *maika* rolling.
Those are games you love."

Yes, Hiku loved the games. He liked to win and
thrilled to hear the shouting. He forgot his longing for
the forest.

But in the night it came. She will not let me go, he
thought. Kāwelu will never let me return to my dear forest. So I shall slip away. Only a few days, to see my family,
to feel the chilly wind and drenching rain, to tramp
among the ferns—only a few days! Then I shall come
back to her. Silently he slipped out of the sleeping house
and found the mountain trail.

Suddenly he heard Kāwelu calling. She had wakened
and was following. "Hiku! Hiku!" she was calling through
the night. She must be taking the rough trail! He heard
but went more quickly. She would not follow far! Soon
she would return to the warm house. She could not keep
him with her all the time. He longed to smell the forest!

Again he heard her calling. She could not climb so
fast as he and her voice was farther off as she chanted:

> "Hiku! O Hiku, come back!
> O my husband, wait for Kāwelu!
> The mountain is steep and rough.
> O Hiku, wait for Kāwelu."

But Hiku did not wait. Silly girl to climb this hard
trail! Soon she would go back. He wanted only a few days
in the upland. Then he would return to her. Already he
could feel the cool touch of the mist and sniff the forest
smells. He must go forward.

Very faint and far away he heard her voice once
more:

"Hiku is climbing the mountain.
Kāwelu is following
Over the rocks, through streams.
It is hopeless to follow.
O Hiku, my husband!
Let us go back together."

Cold rain swept about Hiku. Oh, the welcome of its cold! The joy of struggling through it! But Kāwelu would not like the rain and it would drive her home. Soon he would return to her.

Through the slash of the rain and beat of branches Hiku seemed to hear, still, his wife's voice, faintly calling. Yet he went on.

He spent glorious days in the upland. He rejoiced to see his family. He climbed and tramped. He sang and shouted with the mountain storm. Then, one day, he stood beside his mother looking at the great ocean which lay all about his island. He could see a line of white along the shore and he thought of the glory of riding the surf and hearing the shouting crowd.

Faintly a sound rose to his ears. It was not shouting such as he had heard before. Hiku listened, wondering. "O my mother," he asked at last, "what sound is that?"

She turned sad eyes upon his face. "It is the sound of wailing," she replied. "People are wailing for Kāwelu."

"For Kāwelu? What do you mean?"

"When you left her, her heart was full of grief and fear. She tried to follow you. The trail was hard. She met cold rain and clinging vines. Weary and heartbroken she returned and went to the kingdom of Milu, the land of death. Her people are mourning for their chiefess."

"She is my wife!" Hiku cried. All his love rose up in him. "Why did I leave her? I shall go to her! She cannot stay in that dark land. I shall bring her back to sport and laughter. My love will conquer death!"

His mother saw that he was ready to rush down the mountain. "Wait!" she commanded. "What shall you do?"

Hiku stood still. "I do not know," he answered.

"Talk with your father," she advised. "Talk with mighty Kū, your father."

So Hiku went to Kū. His father spoke at once. "You would go to the land of Milu?" he said. "I know the entrance, the only door by which a living man may enter the land of death. I shall take you there. But you, alone, have caused your wife to enter that dark land and you, alone, must make the plan to rescue her."

Sad thoughts rose up in Hiku. He had done wrong. He had caused Kāwelu to journey to the land of death. Without her, there was no joy in life—no fun in sport and shouting, no happiness in beach or forest. He must plan. There must be a way to bring Kāwelu back!

At last Hiku returned to Kū. He had gathered morning glory vines and twisted them into one long strong rope. On one end he had tied a crosspiece on which he could sit. "I am ready," he told his father.

Together they went to Waipi'o. In a cave Kū showed his son the opening into the land of Milu. "It is dark," Hiku whispered, looking through the hole.

"It seems dark at first," his father answered. "Are you afraid?"

"No!" Hiku straightened up. "Here is my swing of morning glory vine. As I sit on the crosspiece slowly let me down into that land of death. Then wait, holding the vine. I may be long. I may be conquered by death. Then I shall stay with Kāwelu. But if all is well I shall get her with me on the swing. When you feel a quick jerk slowly pull us up and Kāwelu will return to life."

Kū understood. "There is one thing more, my son. How can you, a living man, go safely among the dead?"

"I thought of that," Hiku replied and rubbed his body with the bad-smelling oil of spoiled *kukui* nuts then

dusted himself with earth. "Bad smelling and dirty, no spirit will want to touch me," he told Kū. "If they do not touch me they will not know I am alive."

Kū was satisfied and made ready to let down the swing.

Down into the dark went Hiku but soon the darkness lessened and he could see the spirits walking in that dim land, under its trees and along its trails. He moved among them. They thought him one of them, but drew away from dirt and evil smell. So Hiku went fearlessly, looking and listening. He saw Kāwelu. She sat beside Milu, the chief, on a pile of fine mats. Did Milu hope to take Kāwelu for his wife? He should not have her!

Hiku went to the swing once more. Again he sat on the crosspiece and, pushing with his feet, swung back and forth just as he had swung in childhood.

"My Swing! My Swing!" he chanted,
"A whistling sound it makes as I swing.
I swing! I swing!
You others have no swing!"

The spirits of the land of death heard his chant. They saw the fine motion of the swing and gathered round. "Let me swing!" each one was crying.

"Very well," said Hiku. He stopped the swing and let a spirit have it, then another and another.

"Let me swing too!" That was the voice he waited for! Kāwelu had come and asked to swing.

"It is hard to cling to the vines," said Hiku. "Better that I hold you on my lap. Together we shall go very high."

Kāwelu did not recognize him—did not know the husband whom she loved, here in the land of death! She drew away from him saying, "You are dirty!"

Hiku mounted the swing. "I shall spread my *kapa* over my lap, so. Now sit here while we swing." Almost before she knew, he had her on his lap and in his arms.

They were swinging, higher and higher. And the spirits shouted even as living men had shouted on the beach. " 'Ā! Kāwelu! She goes higher than we have gone!"

Hiku jerked the rope of vines, then tightened his arms about his wife. Still they were swinging back and forth. Only Hiku knew that Kū was slowly pulling up the swing, up toward the light of day.

Suddenly the spirits gave a cry. "They are going up! He is stealing Kāwelu!"

The two were very near the opening. Kāwelu struggled as if she feared the light and life but Hiku held her close. They passed through the opening and came out into the sunlight.

Hiku bent over his dear wife, tears falling on her face. She opened her eyes and smiled at him. "I dreamed!" she whispered. "A terrible dream! You loved the forest better than you loved Kāwelu and you went away from me. In sorrow I, too, went away—down to the land of Milu. It was just a dream!"

"Yes," Hiku told her, "a bad dream!"

But from this "dream" both had learned much. Both played as before upon the beach but when the longing came to Hiku, they went together to the forest. Hiku helped Kāwelu on the trail, he taught her to love the wind and driving rain, to love the mountain sports. Seaside and mountain, Hiku and Kāwelu were together.

Told by Mary Kawena Pūku'i.

The Dream Girl

"**O** Grandmother!"

Old Maka lay on her mats between waking and sleeping. Had she heard a call? "O Grandmother, come and get me!"

The old woman opened her eyes. Beside her bed stood a young woman, tall and very lovely. Maka gazed at her in wonder. "I have never seen you before, beautiful girl," she said at last. "What do you want?"

"O Grandmother, come and get me," the young woman begged again. "I lie on the trash pile beside the gardens. I lie among dry cane stalks and *kalo* leaves. Come quickly before I die!" There were tears in the girl's eyes. Old Maka tried to speak to her again but she was gone.

The old woman roused herself and sat up on her mats. A dream? Yes, it had been a dream, but the call for help was real. The old woman drew a *kapa* about her shoulders and stood a moment in the doorway. Her eyes were full of tears because of the sorrow of the dream girl.

Gray mist of early morning filled the world. Yet somehow the old woman found the path and followed it up to the gardens. The trash pile! Where was the trash pile? Through her tears she saw a rainbow in the mist. She wiped away her tears so that she could see more clearly. And now she saw the rainbow, small and very bright, hanging above the trash pile. She stooped closer. There, among dry stalks of sugar cane and *kalo* leaves, a tiny baby lay. Old Maka took the baby in her arms. She wrapped it in her *kapa* and held it close against her breast for warmth. As she stumbled home her eyes again were full of tears for this child deserted on a trash pile.

When she reached the house the sun had risen and the mist was gone. In the clear warm light old Maka and

her husband looked long at the baby—a beautiful little girl. "A little chiefess," Maka told her husband, "for over her I saw a rainbow, small, but very bright."

"It is the sign of a chiefess," her husband said. "It does not matter who she is. We shall care for the little one."

And so they did. They fed and cared for her and kept her always with them, safe in their upland home. The little girl played with birds and lizards, she swam in the mountain pool, she made *lei* of *lehua* blossoms and danced and sang. But she was always alone except for the old couple. "A chiefess must not mix with common folk," they said and so Nohea, their beautiful girl, never saw young people. She never saw a girl of her own age, nor a young man.

She grew to womanhood and became the lovely woman of Maka's dream. "What now?" the old woman asked her husband. "The time has come for her to marry. Where shall we find a husband for our young chiefess?"

The gods who guarded Nohea had their plan. One night the young woman dreamed. In her dream she saw a man—tall, straight, handsome and wearing a cape of feathers and a feather covering on his head. In his hand was a great stick. Nohea had never seen a warrior. She did not recognize the feather garments nor the war club but she listened to the young man's words. "You must go on a strange journey," he said to her, "a strange, hard journey." Then he was gone.

Nohea woke and thought about her dream. "A strange journey." She did not understand but the forest was in her mind. She seemed to see herself in the cool of the forest. She seemed to see herself pushing her way through tangled growth, resting beside a spring and climbing *lehua* trees to gather blossoms. Nohea thought much that day but she did nothing.

That night she dreamed again. Again the stranger came wearing feather garments. But tonight he did not seem a stranger—rather an old friend. Again he spoke to her. "Make ready for a journey, O Nohea," he said. "You must start at once." The dream ended and the girl awoke.

She sprang up from her mats. I must start at once! she told herself, for the words of the young man were ringing in her ears. She put on her *pā'ū* and shoulder cape but did not stop for food. She went out into the chill of early morning. The thought of the forest was strong in her, again, and she followed the trail that led to it.

For days Nohea wandered in the forest just as her thoughts had pictured. Sometimes she pushed her way through tangled undergrowth. She stumbled over hidden logs, vines caught her feet and her *kapa* was wet with dew. Sometimes she wandered in a sunny, open grove of *lehua*. She gathered blossoms and made *lei* for her neck and hair. She slept beside a spring.

In her sleep the man came to her. He called and beckoned to her. In the day she did not see him but sometimes she saw a rainbow which seemed to wave her onward and she followed. She was not afraid, for she felt her friend was guiding her.

One day she heard loud sounds. Something was crashing through the underbrush, some animal or person. Frightened, Nohea climbed a tree.

A moment later a man came from among the ferns and stood looking at her. "Come down, beautiful girl," he said. His voice was friendly but Nohea was still afraid.

Then the man threw himself down before her. He threw himself down as a man does before his chief. Nohea did not know that custom but she understood that this man would not hurt her. "Come down," he begged again. "O Heavenly One, let me lead you to my master, chief of Kohala. He has seen you in his dreams and he waits for your coming. Let me lead you to him."

Was this the answer to her dream? Was it this chief who had spoken to her? Slowly Nohea climbed down and followed the man who led her out of the forest and along a trail.

At last they came to a group of houses. In the shade young men were busy with some game. The one who led Nohea bowed before the tallest man. "I have found her, O Heavenly One," he said.

The young man turned toward Nohea. His face lighted with great joy as he came to her. "You have come, O woman of my dreams," he said. "But your eyes are full of tears. Why do you weep?"

"I dreamed of someone," she whispered.

"What was he like? Was he like me?"

"Yes, his voice was yours, and his eyes, but he was different. He wore a long cape of feathers. He wore feathers on his head and held a great stick in his hand."

The man turned to his servant. "Bring my feather cape and helmet," he commanded. "Bring my war club."

He put them on. "Behold your warrior!"

Nohea smiled. "My warrior indeed!" she said. "I know you now. It was you who came to me in dreams. Let me send for my old people, the grandparents who cared for me. But for them I should not be alive."

On the day that the chief of Kohala and Nohea were married a great storm covered mountain and plain. Thunder roared and sheets of blinding rain swept down the mountains but the rain was lighted by rainbows.

Old Maka listened to the thunder and watched the rainbows joyfully, then turned to her husband with shining eyes. "The gods are glad," she said. "They send storm and rainbows to celebrate the marriage of the chiefess whom we love."

From Hawaiian Antiquities and Folklore *by Fornander.*

The Hidden Island of 'Ualaka'a

"Today you go fishing far at sea?"

"We go far, O Heavenly One." The two fishermen pointed where the sky rests on the ocean.

"Take me with you."

"Not so, O Heavenly One. What if some evil befall you?"

"There is no danger," Kaēwe said. "Each day you two paddle out to sea for fish and do not think of danger."

"But you, O Heavenly One! You are chief of Waipi'o. Your wise and fair rule is known throughout these islands. Because of you Waipi'o flourishes, men live without fear, there is plenty in our land. No harm must come to you, O Heavenly One!"

"No harm will come!" answered Kaēwe impatiently. "The sky is clear, the ocean smiles and wind blows steadily. What harm could come?"

"There is always danger at sea," one fisherman replied. "A sudden change of wind. A sudden storm. Forgive us, Heavenly One! We cannot take you." The two pushed off their canoe and paddled away while the young chief stood watching in disappointment.

Someone else was watching. Kaēwe's steward had seen how the chief talked with these two fishermen. He had seen this many times and it angered him. "Favorites!" he exclaimed and made an evil plan. It was his work to take food to the chief's men. These men served Kaēwe in many ways: as fishermen, farmers, canoe builders or warriors. To each man's family food was taken daily. "These favorites shall have no food!" the steward said.

After a hard day at sea the fishermen returned to rest and eat. No food! They kept a few small fish from the day's catch. With these they ate leftovers of vegetable food. "Some mistake," they said. "Tomorrow we shall have plenty, for Kaēwe is a generous chief."

But the next night there was still no food. It was so for many nights. The men grew angry. "Auē!" they said. "We refuse to take our chief into danger. He rewards our care of him by ordering no food for us!" They also formed an evil plan.

Next morning the two made ready their canoe before Kaēwe reached the landing place. In the bottom they laid two paddles, then their nets which hid the extra paddles.

"Aloha, O my fishermen!" the chief called as he came near. "This is the day to take me with you."

The fishermen looked at sea and sky. "It shall be so, O Heavenly One," they answered. "The sea smiles and the sky is clear."

The chief's face was full of joy for he loved fishing. He stepped in and settled himself in the canoe, watching the paddles fly. Over the reef they went and out into the ocean swells. He loved the feel of the salt breeze! He was glad the fishermen were going far!

Hawai'i became only a gray, cloud-covered line. "Where are your fishing grounds?" Kaēwe asked.

"Far out where the waves break in white foam. There we shall anchor."

"Are there no fish nearer shore?"

"Only small ones. Out farther lies the canoe of Hina, wife of the fish god."

Kaēwe watched the waves break in the white foam. A sudden cry called his eyes back to the canoe. One man had dropped his paddle. As he reached for it the canoe tipped and all three tried to hold it steady. Somehow, in the excitement, the other paddle was lost. No paddles and far from land! Kaēwe did not need to be told the danger. "I will swim for them," he said, "for I am youngest."

The paddles were drifting away but they had not gone far. The chief jumped in. A few strong strokes and he had one! Then the other!

He turned. His two fisherman were paddling toward shore. "Wait!" Kaēwe shouted. He could not understand what had happened. Where did they get the paddles they were using? Did they mean to leave him? Why?

"Don't leave me!" he shouted. "I shall drown! Save your chief! What have I done to harm you? Tell me and I will make it right. Only save me!" They did not stop or return but paddled on until their canoe was a faint speck on the blue ocean.

Kaēwe swam. He was a strong swimmer but his island was only a distant line of gray. He swam and rested, then swam again. The land seemed no nearer. Was he caught in a current and being carried away forever from his home and people—from life? He swam with all his strength.

Mist gathered about him. It shut out the dim line of Hawai'i. Kaēwe did not know that in that mist a red light glowed and a rainbow hung above him but these signs of a chief were plain to a watcher in the sky.

Now a storm broke. Wind tossed the waves. Kaēwe forgot land and home. He only struggled to keep afloat among those leaping waves.

Then a new sound! It was like the breaking of waves on sand but Kaēwe knew there was no shore near. This must be the sound of a hugh fish—a fish coming to swallow him! He swam with all his strength away from the sound. But a great wave caught him and rolled him onto a beach where he lay motionless.

After a long time he woke again to life. He tried to stand but could only crawl farther from the waves. There he dropped down on the warm sunny sand and slept.

Kaēwe slept long and woke wondering where he was. He got to his feet and looked about him. What island could this be? He remembered the direction the canoe had taken. There should be no island here, and yet—! He was in the most beautiful place he had ever seen. Such great trees, such flowers and such fruit! He came to a garden. Bananas were dropping from their stalks. *Kalo* and sweet potatoes were pushing from the ground. The sight of so much food made his mouth water, for he was very hungry. Whose garden was this? If only he could have a little of this food!

Feeling that he was being watched, Kaēwe turned quickly and saw a young woman peeping at him from the bushes. Wonder and fear were in her face and she looked ready to run. "I have come far," he said, "and am hungry. May I have a little of this food?"

"Not this," she answered. "This is poison. I shall give you food. Follow me." Still half afraid, she led him to a house and brought out berries. "Eat," she said.

Kaēwe tasted the berries. They were not very good and his mind was full of the thought of *kalo,* sweet potatoes and bananas, fresh from the *imu.* "Whose garden is that?" he asked, pointing. "May we not eat some of that food?"

"It is poison," she repeated, "and will kill you, Man-of-the-Sea."

He stared at her. The good vegetables he had seen could not be poison! "They will not hurt us if we cook them," he said at last.

"Cook?" the woman asked. "What does that mean—cook?"

Kaēwe stared again. "Cook in an *imu,*" he repeated. "Don't you cook *kalo,* breadfruit and sweet potatoes?"

The woman only stared. She had never eaten cooked food! What island could this be where gardens were full of food yet people ate only berries? "I shall show you," Kaēwe said.

Then he stood thinking. All his life he had eaten cooked food but he was a chief and had never prepared an *imu,* never made a fire. "But I have seen it done," he thought. Many times he had watched servants do this work and it looked easy.

He hunted for a digging stick, then made a hole and looked for stones. Were those the right sort? He knew some stones would not hold heat and some would burst when heated. Those would not do for an *imu.*

He found plenty of wood and laid it ready. He had seen men rub one stick in the hollowed groove of another to make fire. He found a short stick of hard wood and a flat piece of softer *hau.* Now! Holding the *hau* firmly with his feet, he rubbed quickly back and forth. He made a groove in the *hau* and in it powdered wood. Why did the powder not catch fire? The woman was watching. He must show her he could do this thing.

Smoke at last! Then he lost the smoke. Finally he had a spark. He tried to catch it on a bit of *kapa* torn from his *malo.* The spark was gone and he had to start all over. But he worked steadily. Another spark! Another! The powdered wood was burning and his bit of *kapa.*

He dropped dry leaves and twigs upon the fire. They blazed up in his face, burning his eyebrows and scorching his skin. But the woman was watching! She must not know he had been hurt. He laughed.

With his blazing stick he lighted the wood of the *imu,* then laid the stones where they would heat. He pulled *kalo* and sweet potatoes, picked breadfruit and bananas, washed the vegetables and wrapped them ready for the *imu.* He caught fish in the stream. At last food and hot stones were packed together and the *imu* covered. Kaēwe was proud of his success. He would show this woman what cooking meant! But a servant's work—that was what he had done—a servant's work! And he was chief of Waipiʻo.

Tired from his long swim and hard work he slept once more, this time beside the *imu.* He was wakened by the woman's sobs. As he sat up she stared at him.

"O Man-of-the-Sea, I thought that you had died," she sobbed. "I thought your hard work had killed you!"

Kaēwe laughed. "I must finish my work," he said. He opened the *imu,* broke a breadfruit and laid a steaming piece on a large leaf. When it had cooled a little he put it before the woman.

He took another piece for himself. Oh, the good smell! He broke off a bit but before he could put it into his mouth the woman struck his arm so that he dropped the food. "Don't!" she cried. "Don't eat it! It will kill you! O Man-of-the-Sea I do not want you to die."

Kaēwe looked at the young woman in great wonder.

She was weeping. She was weeping for him because she thought cooked breadfruit would kill him!

"Do not cry," he said gently. "This is the food I am used to. I have eaten it all my life. It has made me tall and strong—this cooked food. See." In spite of her weeping he tasted the breadfruit, then thought of nothing but the food. Banana, fish, sweet potatoes! How good it all tasted! In his hunger he almost forgot the woman. She was weeping now but watching every mouthful that he ate.

At last his hunger was satisfied. As he leaned back against a tree to look at the young woman he almost laughed at the wonder in her face. "That was good!" he said. "I feel better. Taste the breadfruit, Woman-of-the-Island."

Very much afraid, she took a tiny taste—another—and another. "It is good," she said. "I hope it does not kill me."

"It won't," Kaēwe told her. "It will make you even more beautiful. Tell me your name, O Woman-of-the-Island, and tell me the name of this island where you live."

"I am Ka'analike," she replied, "high chiefess of this island of 'Ualaka'a."

'Ualaka'a? Suddenly Kaēwe understood. This was an island of the gods, one of the hidden islands of Kāne. He had never heard that any living man had set foot on one of those islands. Yet he was here, alive, breathing the

perfumed air, drinking in beauty such as man had never seen and eating the fruit of this land. Kaēwe was filled with wonder.

For days he served the chiefess, Ka'analike. "Have you no servants?" he asked her. "Are you all alone on this beautiful island?"

"Oh no!" she told him. "My parents and our servants have gone to gather berries in the mountains. Berries are our food." She laughed. "They once were my food before the coming of Man-of-the-Sea."

One day Ka'analike told Kaēwe that her parents would soon return. "I must hide you," she said, "for they may be angry at sight of a stranger." So Kaēwe was hidden when the parents and their servants came.

"What are you eating, daughter?" Kaēwe heard the father's question.

"*Kalo*—cooked *kalo*. It is very good."

"It is poison," the father answered.

"No so," replied Ka'analike. "Do I look ill?"

"You grow more beautiful each day," he told her.

"Because of this new food. For many days I have eaten cooked vegetables. Come with me." She showed her parents the wonders of the *imu* and explained how food was cooked by the heat of stones. They tasted the cooked food and liked it.

"But who has taught you these new ways?" her mother asked.

"Man-of-the-Sea. Perhaps he was sent by Kāne. He can make sticks blossom with fire and the fire heats the stones for cooking. Man-of-the-Sea is very wise."

The father looked about wondering. "He must be both wise and good," he said. "Surely he was sent by Kāne. Where is this man of wisdom?"

Then Ka'analike knew she need not hide Kaēwe any longer. As she called him out she told her parents,

"Man-of-the-Sea has been a servant to me. Let him be so no longer. Let him teach our servants the art of cooking. O Father, O Mother, I would have Man-of-the-Sea for my husband!"

"Your marriage is not in our hands, O Ka'analike," her father answered. "You may not choose a husband without the permission of your grandfather."

"And my grandfather is high chief in the land of the sky, in the deep blue of heaven!" the young chiefess said. "O my father, how can I reach him? How can I ask him?"

The father drew out a large wooden bowl. "In this lives the sacred coconut," he told her. "You have only to climb this sacred tree and you will reach the deep blue of heaven. Are you ready?"

"I am ready," Ka'analike answered.

The father carried the calabash into the yard and took off the cover. Inside was a small coconut tree. As the cover was taken off the tree began to grow. Ka'analike leaped onto the growing trunk and in a moment perched among the leaves. Up and up grew the tree—higher and higher until its top touched the deep blue of heaven. Then Ka'analike saw an opening and a moment later was in the land of her grandfather.

She followed a trail and came face to face with an old man who wore a feather cape and an ivory neck orna-ment, signs of a chief. "*Aloha,* Grandfather!" she said.

The old man looked long at the young chiefess. "You must be Ka'analike," he made answer. "What important matter brings you to the sky, my child?"

"The matter of my marriage," she replied. "A stranger came to 'Ualaka'a. He came from the sea. O my grandfather, I would have this man for my husband."

"It is well," the old man answered. "I saw this one swimming in the sea. About him was a glowing mist and above him hung a rainbow. Signs of a chief, I thought.

A fit husband for Ka'analike, and I rolled 'Ualaka'a toward him and saw a wave lift him to its beach. Go back, my child, and take him for your husband."

So Kaēwe and Ka'analike were married. There were days of feasting, games and *hula*. Kaēwe was high chief of the hidden island of 'Ualaka'a. His days were spent in ease with his lovely wife. In that island of beauty and plenty they were very happy—for there was never sickness, hunger nor want. Hawai'i was only a dim memory to Kaēwe.

Then he had a strange dream. In his dream he was again in Waipi'o. He walked about his valley and saw that his people no longer honored their gods. He saw neglected gardens, broken buildings and dirty streams and springs. His people did not work and hunger and sickness were on every hand. He saw his father and mother and heard them weep. He knew they mourned for him.

The dream faded and Kaēwe woke. But his heart was heavy for the suffering of his people was in his mind. Games, music, even the love of his beautiful wife could not drive away the memory of that dream.

The dream came again and yet again. Kaēwe's heart was very sad. Waipi'o needed him. His people mourned for him. He was alive and strong but knew not how to return to Hawai'i.

Ka'analike saw her husband's sorrow. "What has happened?" she asked. "Are you not happy in 'Ualaka'a?"

"Life is good here," he replied, "but in my island of Hawai'i there is want and suffering. The people need their chief. I am that chief. You call me Man-of-the-Sea, but I am from Waipi'o on the island of Hawai'i. My name is Kaēwe. My people need me and I cannot return."

"Is Hawai'i more beautiful than 'Ualaka'a?" she asked. "Do the birds sing more sweetly? Are the flowers brighter or the people more wise and good?"

"Not so," he answered. "'Ualaka'a is more beautiful than any island in the world I came from. But in Waipi'o they have need of me."

Tears came to the eyes of the young chiefess. "Do not leave me, Man-of-the-Sea," she said.

"My love for you is great," he told her, "but Hawai'i calls me."

Then Ka'analike ordered her men to build a canoe. It was built in a single day. Its sails were red and each paddler wore a red *malo* and red *lei*. As the red light of sunset fell upon 'Ualaka'a the canoe was launched. Ka'analike looked her last upon the husband whom she loved. "You sail to Hawai'i," she said, "to those who need you. Do not look back."

He was gone. She rolled her sacred island after his canoe until she saw the waves breaking on Hawai'i. Then she rolled the island away into the mist. She would never look upon Man-of-the-Sea again.

Men of Waipi'o saw a canoe sail out of the sunset. It came to the chief's landing. Suddenly a shout went up: "Kaēwe! It is Kaēwe! He has come home!"

Men rushed to meet the canoe. They lifted it. Chief, paddlers and all, they lifted it, and carried it to the chief's own yard. Kaēwe stepped out. Tears were in his eyes. "*Aloha*, O my people!" he said. "I have come home." Then he went to greet his parents.

Order and industry came again to Waipi'o. Men prayed and worked and soon the gardens were full of food. The song of *kapa* beaters sounded in the village and the song of adzes in the forest. Holidays came and men and women joined in games and *hula*.

For Kaēwe the hidden island of 'Ualaka'a and its lovely chiefess were but a dim memory. Could any island be more beautiful than Hawai'i? Or any valley dearer than Waipi'o that needed him?

From Hawaiian Legends *by Rice, used by permission of Bishop Museum Press, Bernice Pauahi Bishop Museum.*

The Kī-Leaf Trumpet

"In all the world there is no chiefess more lovely than Lāʻie, the Beauty of Paliuli."

The story teller spoke softly but the sisters who were listening cried out in excitement: "Have you seen her?"

"Where does she live?"

"I want to see her!"

"You cannot," the storyteller answered. "Paliuli is in a deep forest high on the mountainside in Hawaiʻi. There her grandmother has hidden Lāʻie and built for her a house thatched with golden feathers."

"Oh, we must see her!" the sisters cried. "Let us go there. We can climb the mountain."

"You cannot go," the storyteller said again. "The forest is very thick. Branches will tear your clothes and vines will trip you. No one can go to Paliuli."

"We can," the oldest sister said. "Perhaps no common person can climb to that hidden land but we are daughters of a chief. We do not fear the forest nor the mountain. What do you say, Hala Blossom?" The four sisters turned to the youngest.

"I want to hear more about her," replied Hala Blossom softly.

"She lives alone with her grandmother and her old nurse," the storyteller continued.

"But she must have servants!"

"Her servants are birds. She rests on the wings of birds."

"How beautiful!"

"But lonely!" Hala Blossom said. "No friends! Only a grandmother and old nurse! And we are five—five sisters to laugh and talk and sing together. Let us go to the Beauty of Paliuli, for she must be very lonely."

The sisters planned, then told their family. "It is no use to go," everyone said. "The mountain is high, the forest deep. Even if you should reach the home of the young chiefess you cannot see her for she stays inside her golden-feathered house. If ever she goes out she is hidden by thick mist."

"But she will let us in," the sisters said. "She must be lonely and will welcome us."

"No," they were told. "She lets no one in. You may call and call but her door will never open."

"Perhaps no one else has been invited in," the oldest sister said, "but we also are daughters of a chief. She will welcome us. Let us make ready for the journey."

So the five sisters set out from Kaua'i to Hawai'i. They reached the Puna coast. There they left their canoe and asked the way to Paliuli. Then they climbed. The climb was long but the girls were strong and eager. Up and up they went. They reached the forest. There it was damp and dark but the sisters were not afraid.

The trees grew thicker, vines tripped them, bushes scratched their arms and legs, they stumbled over logs. Still they went bravely on. "We are daughters of a chief," they said. "We cannot turn back."

They found berries which they ate and felt new strength. On and up they went through the thick forest. One stumbled and fell, the others helped her up. One cut her foot on a sharp stone but she found healing leaves and bound up her wound. She too went bravely on.

When darkness came the girls crowded together inside a hollow tree. The forest was damp and cold and they slept in each other's arms, trying to keep warm. The night was very long.

Morning at last! Stiff and tired the sisters crawled out of their hollow tree. "Look!" cried Hala Blossom. They turned to look where she pointed and held their breath in wonder. A long ray of the morning sun fell upon a house. It was thatched with tiny golden feathers—more beautiful than a dream.

For a moment no one spoke. Then one said softly, "We are here. This is Paliuli."

The girls found a spring and bathed. They combed their hair and fastened blossoms in it. Each put on a fresh *pāʻū* in place of the one torn by the forest climb. Then they stood at the edge of the garden and called:

> "O Beauty of Paliuli,
> We have come.
> In far Kauaʻi we heard of you,
> The loveliest chiefess of all the world.
> We have come.
> Over the ocean we paddled.
> Up the mountain we climbed.
> Through the forest we searched.
> Our clothes were torn.
> Our feet were scratched.
> Yet we have come.
> We are five sisters.
> We too are daughters of a chief.
> We have come to your golden-feathered house.
> O Beauty of Paliuli,
> Let us in
> That we may look upon your loveliness."

So they called and waited. There was no answer. The door of that golden-feathered house was closed. The sisters went back into the forest. They hunted berries and drank from the spring then sat in a sunny place to make some plan.

The oldest sister spoke. "Each of us has a sacred perfume," she said, "as mine is the perfume of the *maile* that grows in the heavens. Tonight I will go to the golden-feathered house and my perfume will slip through the thatch. It will waken the young chiefess and she will call us in."

Darkness came and sweet smells filled the air. At midnight the oldest sister entered the garden and stood beside the house. She knew her perfume filled the garden. She knew it slipped through the feather thatch into the house. Then she heard a soft voice call, "Grandmother! O Grandmother!"

"Yes, my child," came the answer in a sleepy voice. "Why do you waken me at midnight?"

"I smell a sweet perfume. What is it?"

"It is the *maile* perfume of the oldest sister, one of those who came from Kaua'i to see you."

"One of those who called to me?" The soft voice was laughing. "Another trick to see me! Let them go away! I shall not see them!" All was quiet. The oldest sister heard no more. She knew the young chiefess slept and her plan had failed.

The next night the second sister stood beside the house and her perfume filled the air. The soft voice called, "Grandmother! O Grandmother!"

"What is it, child? Why do you waken me at midnight?"

"The perfume, Grandmother. This is different but very sweet. It fills the house. What is it?"

"It is the perfume of the second sister," the old voice answered, "the second chiefess from Kaua'i."

"One of those who called?" Another trick to see me! Let those sisters go back to Kaua'i for I will not see them!"

The third sister tried and the fourth but the words of the young chiefess were always the same, "Let them go away. I will not see them."

"Yet she is lonely," Hala Blossom said. "She must be lonely. She must long for friends, only she does not know. She does not understand the longing in her heart."

"Then you will try," the sisters said. "Tonight you will stand beside the door. Your *hala*-blossom perfume is very strong and sweet. She will open the door for you."

"No," Hala Blossom answered slowly, "I have another plan. After the sun sets let us build a fire. The young chiefess will see it and wonder who is in the forest. She may come out to see."

"She may come out," the oldest sister said, "but she may not."

"That is not all my plan. In the night you shall sing—you, the oldest of us. Your voice is sweet as the voice of a snail singing before the dawn. Surely Lāʻie will come out to hear you better."

That night the sisters sat around their fire. They heaped on wood and kept it burning brightly. At midnight the oldest sister sang. She sang long and sweetly. Her song died away on the night air but there was no answer from the house.

The next morning the girls were very sad. "We have tried everything," they said. "Let us go home."

"No!" cried Hala Blossom. "Are we not daughters of a chief! Let us try again. Tonight we shall build another fire. Tonight our second sister is the one to sing."

They agreed. The voice of the second sister floated on the breeze but no sound came from the house where Lāʻie lived. Still Hala Blossom would not give up. Each night the girls sat about their fire and each night one sister sang.

"Your turn has come," the older girls told Hala Blossom. "This plan is yours and tonight you are the one to sing."

The youngest took something from behind her ear. "I have made a kī-leaf trumpet," she said. "Tonight I shall sound that."

As darkness fell the girls lighted their fire. While the flames danced into the darkness Hala Blossom sounded her kī-leaf trumpet. She played a merry tune that danced with the flames but there was no answer from the chiefess's house. At last Hala Blossom lay down and slept.

Before dawn she wakened. She pulled her *kī*-leaf trumpet from behind her ear and sounded it once more.

She played a lonely call as if one cried for help. Then she played a merry tune—a laughing echo to her call. Still there was no answer from the home of Lā‘ie.

Daylight came and the sun sent slanting rays upon the golden-feathered house. The oldest sister rose. "It is enough," she said. "We have tried every plan. Let us go home."

"Not yet!" Hala Blossom answered. "I will not give up. The young chiefess longs for friends though she does not understand the longing in her heart. When she hears us sing and play she longs for us. It may be tonight she will give way to her longing. It may be tonight she will send for us."

So once more the fire was built and the sisters sat around it. They listened as Hala Blossom played her merry, dancing tune. "It is fine and sweet," said one, but the young chiefess sleeps." Before dawn Hala Blossom sounded her *kī*-leaf trumpet once again but her sisters heard no answer.

They were tired and silent. Their fire died. Daylight grew, but the sisters still sat around the ashes of their fire, each busy with sad thoughts.

"*Aloha!*" The girls looked up in great surprise. For many days they had been in the forest and seen no one. Now an old hunchback woman stood near and greeted them.

They rose quickly to their feet. "You are welcome," said the oldest. "Sit here with us. If you are cold, we can make up the fire."

"I cannot sit," the old woman made answer. "I come from my young chiefess who lives there." She pointed to the house shining golden in the morning sun. Then she turned toward Hala Blossom. "You are the one who made sweet music before dawn," she said. "I watched you from the darkness of the garden. My young chiefess asks that you come to her. She wants to see your instrument and hear you sound it."

"I will come." Hala Blossom spoke quietly but the hearts of all five sisters were singing with joy and excitement.

Hala Blossom followed the old nurse until she stood before the open door. In the softly lighted house she saw Lā‘ie resting on the wings of birds. On her shoulder perched birds of royal red. They held *lehua* blossoms above her and shook drops of dew which made a rainbow on her hair. And the face of the young chiefess! She was more lovely than a dream. Hala Blossom fell on her face before such beauty.

"What is the matter?" the old nurse asked. "Come to my young chiefess."

"I cannot," the girl whispered. "She is so beautiful, so wonderful! I cannot come before her."

But Lā‘ie had heard voices. "Have you come, nurse?" she called. "Have you brought the little girl who makes the merry music? Let her come in." The voice was warm and kind. Hala Blossom rose and entered.

"Are you the one who made that merry music in the night?" the young chiefess asked, and the welcome in her voice took away all the girl's fear.

"Yes." Hala Blossom took the *kī*-leaf trumpet from her ear. "I sounded this, O Heavenly One."

"Make your merry tune once more." So Hala Blossom sounded her little trumpet and Lā‘ie laughed with joy.

"Let me try," she said, taking the instrument. She put it to her lips and blew but no sound came. "It is your child," she said as she gave it back. "Stay with me. Every night you shall make music for me."

Hala Blossom heard love in Lā‘ie's voice. She saw love and longing in her eyes and her own love rose to meet that of the lonely chiefess. "I would stay with you gladly, gladly, O Heavenly One," she said, "but I cannot stay in your golden-feathered house while my sisters sleep in a hollow tree."

Lā'ie raised her voice. "Grandmother!" she called. Another old woman came. She was tall and straight and the eyes she turned on Hala Blossom were very keen.

"Grandmother," said the young chiefess, "these five sisters have come from Kaua'i. Four are waiting in the forest. They have sweet perfume and the voices of birds. I would have them for companions."

The old woman seemed to look straight into Hala Blossom's thoughts where she saw love and loyalty. "It is well," she said. "Let them come tonight. Their house shall be ready."

Such excitement when Hala Blossom returned to her sisters! Such happy talk and laughter! Such bathing at the spring and combing out of hair! Such decking with many flower *lei!*

At sunset the girls went to the house of the young chiefess, which glowed softly in the dying light. There they saw her. The four fell on their faces before her beauty but the youngest ran to her with loving greeting.

The chiefess took Hala Blossom in her arms. "My little sister!" she said softly. "All day I have thought of your coming. Bring the others in."

To them she said, "You shall live with me. We shall be six girls together. My grandmother has already built a house for you." Indeed the house was ready, furnished with mats and bowls and *kapa.*

So they lived. They spent their time in such work as daughters of a chief may do. They laughed and talked together and taught Lā'ie songs and stories. They ate food brought to them by birds. Their dream had come true for Paliuli had become their home, a place beloved.

From The Hawaiian Romance of Laieikawai *by Haleole,*
translated by Beckwith.

A Kite and a Toy Canoe

“**I** have seen your picture in the clouds, my brother, and I know that you are sick. What is your sickness?” Halemano's sister bent anxiously above him as he lay upon his mats.

“I am sick with longing for my dream girl,” the young man answered and his voice was very faint. “Every night she comes to me. We wander together under the *lehua* trees and surf together in the rolling waves. But in the morning she is gone. O my sister, I long to see this girl in more than dreams! I long to have her for my wife but I know not where to find her.”

“Tell me of her, Halemano,” the sister said. “Tell me of her look and dress.”

“She is tall, straight and very beautiful,” the young man answered. “Even now I seem to smell the *hala*-blossom perfume of her *kapa*, I seem to see the *lehua lei* about her neck.”

“*Lehua* is a flower of Hawai‘i,” the sister said, “and *hala*-blossom perfume is used in Puna. Has this dream girl never told her name?”

“When I wander by her side I know her name,” the brother answered. “But when I wake, it has gone from me. Oh, help me, sister! Help me to find this girl.”

“Does she come to you whenever you are sleeping?”

“Yes. If I should sleep now she would come.”

“Perhaps I shall hear you talking with her,” the sister said. “Sleep, Halemano.”

With a sigh the young man closed his eyes. Then the sadness left his face. His lips moved as if he talked with someone but the words were very low. His sister bent close to listen. She heard him whisper, “Puna.” She had been right. This dream girl lived in Puna. If only he would say her name! Halemano was not talking now but his face was full of joy. The sister watched and listened. At last she heard words whispered low, "Farewell, Kama. Tonight we—"

His voice faded away but the sister had heard enough. She brought food to her brother as he woke. "Eat," she said. "I shall go to Puna and learn more of this dream girl. Then I shall take you to her. You must eat and grow strong."

Halemano trusted his sister and was full of hope. He ate and drank and soon his sickness left him.

After some days the young woman returned to O'ahu. "It is good that you are strong once more," she said, "for we must journey to Puna on Hawai'i. I learned about this Kama whom you love. She is the beautiful young chiefess of Puna. Because of her beauty her parents keep her hidden from the world. Only a young brother lives with her, a little boy whom Kama loves with all her heart."

"Let us go at once to Puna!" Halemano said eagerly. "I cannot wait to see her."

"Wait a little," the sister answered. "Wait until the toys are finished."

"Toys?"

"Yes, a kite, a small canoe of red with red mat sail and little figures of people painted red and black. I have asked woodcarvers to make them. Let me tell you my plan."

Some days later the two sailed for Puna in a single canoe. They stopped close to a point of land. "This is a good place to fly the kite," the sister said. "The wind is steady. The kite will rise high and be seen by people on the bay where Kama lives."

While she paddled gently Halemano flew the kite. Up and up it went. They heard shouting and the sister paddled round the point of land into the bay. A crowd had gathered on the beach and people looked and pointed. "They never saw a kite before!" said Halemano.

"There is the child," his sister whispered as a small boy waded toward them. The boy was stretching out his hands and calling to them.

The sister paddled closer. Now they could understand what the child was saying, "Give it to me! I want that thing that flies!" They paddled to him and Halemano put the kite string in his hand. The child shouted with joy as he felt it tug. He waded to shore and ran with the kite along the beach while all the people shouted.

Halemano and his sister watched him for a time then launched the toy canoe where a gentle wind would blow it toward the beach. After a time the boy noticed it. Then he lost interest in his kite, gave the string to another and waded out into the bay. "Oh, the small red canoe!" he shouted. "Let me have it!"

"It is yours," said Halemano. The child picked it up to examine the tiny paddles, red ropes and tiny bailer. Then he played with it at the water's edge.

A long time passed while Halemano and his sister waited quietly. They had brought out some small carved figures and set them up in the canoe so the boy should see them. At last he did. "Oh, the little men!" he shouted. "Little men of black and red! Will you give me those, also?" He waded toward the canoe.

"Is your sister fond of you?" Halemano asked.

"Oh yes," the child replied. "She does everything I ask. She is very good to me."

"Then ask her to come here."

The boy waded quickly to the shore. They saw him running toward his home, still holding the toy canoe. They heard him shout, "O Kama, come with me! See my small canoe! And there are little men, as well! The people will give them to me if only you will come."

The two watched anxiously as Kama joined her brother. Was this the girl of Halemano's dream? She took the child's hand and the two came running to the beach and waded out toward the canoe. "It is Kama!" Halemano whispered joyously.

At the same moment the girl must have recognized Halemano, for she stopped and looked long at him. The child was pulling at her hand. "Come!" he repeated eagerly.

Then Kama came quickly to the canoe. She helped her little brother to climb in, climbed lightly in herself and turned for a last look at Puna. "*Aloha* to our parents," she called to the wondering people. "Tell them we are safe. We go with Halemano, my dream companion. He has come to take me to O'ahu. We shall be man and wife."

From Hawaiian Antiquities and Folklore *by Fornander.*

The God of Love

Kānekoa sat with his head between his knees, thinking bitter thoughts. "Lazy one! Idle one!" That was all he heard at home.

He and his young wife had lived content. Their home was good, their garden flourished and there was food in plenty. Then his wife's parents had come. Kānekoa had worked harder. He had made a larger garden, raised more vegetables and caught more fish so that there still was food in plenty. But his wife's mother was never satisfied. She wanted him to work harder—to bring home more sweet potatoes, pound more *poi* and catch more fish. More? More would spoil! Why have more food than was needed?

But she was always shouting, "Lazy one! Idle one!" No matter how hard Kānekoa worked that woman was never satisfied. And now they have turned me out! he thought angrily. They have turned me out of my own home. They have driven me away from the garden I made. They say they will get another husband for the wife I love. When Kānekoa thought of his beautiful young wife tears filled his eyes.

"You seem sad, my friend. What is the matter?"

Kānekoa looked up in great surprise, for he had thought he was alone. He looked into the face of a young man. It was the face of a stranger but very kind. Kānekoa had not meant to tell anyone that his wife's parents had driven him from home. He was ashamed that it was so. Yet now he told it all. "That woman calls me good-for-nothing!" he said. "She wants me to work and work without stopping."

The stranger laughed, but not as if he were making fun of Kānekoa. Rather he laughed as if Kānekoa's troubles would soon be over. "I know you are not lazy and idle," the stranger said. "Come with me to my cave. I shall give you work to do."

He led Kānekoa a little way from the trail. They passed through a good garden—*kalo*, sweet potatoes, banana, *'awa.* It seemed as if the good plants crowded each other.

"Let us pull *kalo*," the stranger said. "Then you shall heat the *imu.* You shall pound the *poi.*"

The work went well. Kānekoa felt strong and pulled big *kalo* roots easily. Wood was ready for the *imu,* the stones were good and the *kalo* was soon cooked. Never had a *poi* pounder seemed so light. Never had Kānekoa pounded *poi* so quickly nor so well.

The stranger brought fish and the two ate. There was much food left. "You and I are friends," the young man said. "You must trust me and do everything I tell you. Go down to the trail, call to passing travelers and ask them to come and eat. Bring them here and put food before them."

Kānekoa was a generous man and the words of his new companion seemed very good. He forgot his own sorrow in this new work. Each day he labored in the garden, each day he prepared food. He called to hungry travelers and many came gladly to the cave to eat.

Some of the travelers were neighbors whom Kānekoa had known in Ka‘ū. "This is a good life you lead," they said to him. "Here you have a pleasant home and food in plenty. You are well rid of that scolding woman!" "She is going to get a new son-in-law," one neighbor said. "She is planning to marry your wife to that young wrestler."

So! That woman would bring another man to live in houses that I built! She would give him my garden! She would give him my wife! She cannot do that. No other man shall have the wife I love! These were his thoughts, but what could Kānekoa do?

A few days later his companion said, "Your wife's parents have heard that you are here. Today they are coming to find you. The young wrestler is coming with them, for they have asked him to kill you so that your wife will marry him."

Kānekoa was filled with anger and with fear. If only he could fight that wrestler! But he could not. He would be killed. "I must go away," he said at last.

"Not so!" his companion answered. "Go on with your work as usual. If the young wrestler attacks you climb the tree beside the cave mouth."

"Tree!" exclaimed Kānekoa. "There is no—" He stopped for he had seen a strange look in his companion's face. Who was this man? Surely he was one to be obeyed.

Kānekoa was busy in the cave when his wife's parents came. He was feeding a company of tired travelers who sat and talked as they ate. Suddenly they heard that angry voice. "Come out, lazy one!" it cried.

Kānekoa left his guests and went outside the cave. "So this is where you are!" the woman shouted. "You are taking another's garden! You are using another's home! Too lazy to build houses for yourself."

Kānekoa saw the young wrestler rushing toward him with club upraised. Kānekoa turned toward the cave. His companion was gone but where he had been a great tree stood. Kānekoa leaped into it and the tree seemed to shelter him in its arms.

Then he heard voices. It seemed that the tree called and hundreds of voices answered, "Here we are! Here we are!"

Then …! Kānekoa's feet were on the ground. There was no tree there. Only his friend and companion stood beside him. The companion smiled and pointed where Kānekoa's parents-in-law were running down the trail. The young wrestler was running even faster! Suddenly

Kānekoa threw himself on his face before his companion, for now he understood this was a god.

Still the two lived together in the cave. The companion must be a god, but a god who was very kind. It was his will that Kānekoa prepare food for hungry travelers. And now more travelers were coming. "There is no other place where food is plentiful," they said. "No rain has fallen in Ka'ū. Our gardens are dry and bare."

"Soon your parents-in-law will come, and your wife," Kānekoa's companion said. "Give food to your wife but drive away the others."

"But if they are hungry! I cannot let them starve." The young man knew what hunger was.

"She called you lazy, idle, good-for-nothing," his companion said.

"I know," Kānekoa answered, "but if they weep with hunger—!"

They came and now the woman spoke gently. "Good son," she said, "you have always been kind to your parents. Give us food."

Kānekoa looked into the face of his dear wife. She was pale and weak from hunger and he led her to the cave. The parents would have followed but the great tree stood again before the cave mouth. As the parents tried to enter the cave the tree's branches drove them back.

Every day Kānekoa's wife came. He gave her food and saw her grow strong, plump and rosy as she used to be. The two had happy hours together. If only her parents would leave our home! Kānekoa thought. Then life would be very good.

One day the parents came again, so weak that they could hardly crawl. "Kānekoa," the mother said, "we suffer because of my wrongdoing. I drove you out with lying, cruel words. What shall I do?"

Suddenly Kānekoa's companion stood beside him. He was tall and handsome, a young god. "You can go away," he said sternly. "Go back to your own home and leave Kānekoa and his wife in peace."

The parents had fallen on their faces. Now they crawled away. The young god, with Kānekoa and his wife, watched them go slowly down the trail until they were out of sight. Then the god spoke. "They will leave your home," he said, "and go back where they belong."

"They are sick with hunger," Kānekoa whispered. He was sorry for the old people and wanted to help them.

The god smiled, for he knew Kānekoa's thoughts. "You are right, my friend," he answered. "Take them food." So Kānekoa carried food to his wife's parents, forgetting the woman's angry words. The two never returned to spoil the peace of Kānekoa's home. The young man worked well, as he always had, and there was food in plenty.

It was not long before hungry travelers learned of that food. Kānekoa and his wife fed the hungry and cared for sick and tired ones. "Our god is the god of love," they said. "He helped us and left us to do his work."

Told to Mary Kawena Pūkuʻi by her grandmother.

The Gift of Kū

The great gods sometimes took the form of men and walked about our islands. So it was that Kū married a woman of Hawai'i and settled down, as a common man, to farm the land and raise a family.

Years passed and famine came. All up and down the land people were sick with hunger. Kū's children begged for food and their mother wept. "I can get food for them," the husband said, "but it will mean a long, long journey."

"You will return?" she asked him anxiously.

"If I go, I never shall return," he answered.

She clung to him. "Oh, do not go," she said. But when the children cried and begged for food she came to him again. "I cannot bear to see them suffer," was all she said. Kū understood.

That evening he called her to come out into the yard. He said a sad farewell then, as she watched, stood on his head and sank into the ground. His wife wept bitterly. Each day her tears fell on that place.

At last a shoot pushed from the ground. It grew and soon became a tree with leaves and buds. Quickly the buds swelled and fruit grew and ripened. "This is your father's gift," she told her children.

The *imu* was heated and the ripe fruit cooked. It proved good food. Now there was plenty in that house, plenty to share with neighbors. But only the family of Kū could pick that fruit. If another reached for it the tree drew back and shrank into the ground.

When sprouts appeared the family broke them off and carried them to friends and neighbors. "Plant these," they said, "so you also shall have food." In that way the breadfruit tree was spread throughout Hawai'i.

From The Legend of Kawelo and Other Hawaiian Folktales
by Green and Pūku'i.

The Man Who Always Wore a *Kīhei*

Kalei sat on a rock watching the breakers roll up onto the beach. The wind drove great waves against the rocks and onto sands of Waipiʻo as if it sought to tear away the shore. It tossed the girl's hair and snatched at her as if to carry her, too, far from Hawaiʻi. But Kalei was not afraid. She loved the wind and breaking waves and shouted a song to their rhythm.

"No one would come with me," she thought. "The girls were all afraid. They said I'd get no shellfish but I shall. After a great wave the water is sucked far out. ʻĀ! There are shellfish! Big ones!"

The girl let another wave rush up and break. Then as it swept out she sprang onto the sand, snatched a handful of shellfish and was upon her rock before the next wave swirled about it. Again and again she did this, shouting with the excitement of her dangerous game.

And then—! A clump of shellfish did not come easily from its rock. A moment too long she jerked at it and the next moment found herself seized by a wave, rolled, tossed and swept away! She knew nothing more.

When she woke she was lying on the sand with sunshine warm upon her. Someone had saved her from that wave! Someone was bending over her—a stranger with a kind and friendly face. "You live, Kalei!" he said. "I feared you had gone to the kingdom of Milu." He brought fresh water in her gourd and found her gourd of shellfish.

Kalei watched him wonderingly. "You saved my life," she whispered as he helped her to her feet.

"I am glad of that," he answered. "Do not come for shellfish when the waves are high. Yet I would have you come here often that I may see you." Kalei started home,

then turned to wave farewell, but he was gone. It seemed as if the sea itself had swallowed him.

He came again many times. They swam together when the waves were gentle or sat upon the rock to talk and sing when waves dashed high. Kalei was happy in his companionship and longed to show him to Waipi'o friends. Yet when others surfed or played upon the beach—at those times the stranger never came.

After long companionship Kalei's friend became her husband. Each night he came to her home bringing fish and shellfish for the family but every morning he went away. "Where does he come from?" the father asked.

"Why does he not help us in our farming?" questioned the brothers.

Kalei's only answer was, "I neither know nor care where he comes from. He is strong and loving. That is enough. And why should he help with the farming when he brings sea food for us all?"

For many days the girl was happy in his love. Then, one morning, she woke to find him bending over her with sadness in his face. "Kalei," he whispered, "I must leave you."

Frightened by his tone she sat up quickly. "You will come back?" she asked him. "Tonight you will come home?"

"No, Kalei," he answered with deep sadness, "I can never return. O wife of mine, you have never questioned, never doubted me! Now you must know. I am chief of the sharks and must return to those I rule. I have had happy days with you, days that can be no more. But a child will come. If our child should be a boy he will have a shark's mouth on his back and when he is older can be either shark or man at will. O Kalei, guard him well that he be not an evil shark! Keep the shark's mouth hidden lest people come to fear our son. And feed our boy on fish and vegetable food—no meat. O Kalei, never meat!" He took her in his arms and held her close. Then he was gone and Kalei's heart was empty.

But the child came to fill her life with joy. He was a beautiful baby boy and his mother wrapped him in fine *kapa* which hid the shark's mouth on his back. She told her family her husband's words but from the neighbors hid the nature of Nanaue, her little son.

As he grew she kept him always with her, dressed in *malo* and *kīhei,* or shoulder cape. While still a tiny boy he learned to swim and splashed happily in the pool near his home. Kalei was always close by on the rocks, watching him and holding his *kīhei.* As he grew old enough to run about she taught him never to be without it.

As a baby boy he had eaten with his mother in the woman's eating house but now that he was older he went to eat with grandfather and uncles. "Remember my husband's words," she said to them.

Very soon the boy noticed food which the others did not share with him. "What is that?" he asked, pointing. "Give me some."

His grandfather pulled off a chunk of pork and would have given it to the child but the uncles stopped him. "Remember!" they said to him. "Remember the father's warning." Nanaue looked from one to another, wondering, but said no more.

But some days later, when his uncles were away, he asked his grandfather, "May I have some of that good food? Only a little."

"Yes," the old man answered. "It will make you strong and brave." He placed a bit before the boy. Then, seeing his enjoyment, gave him more. Often after that, when the uncles were away, the boy had meat.

Years passed and Nanaue became a tall and handsome youth. He was well built and strong but solitary because of the need of covering his back. He dared not wrestle with others, never swam among them and often worked alone in Kalei's garden when others were at their games.

These solidary ways were noticed. "Why does Nanaue never join the games?" one person asked another.

"He is strong and works well in his mother's garden."

"But why work all the time and never join the games? That is strange for a young man."

"And his *kīhei*," another added wondering. "A shoulder cape is for warmth when the evening wind blows cold. Yet Nanaue wears his when he works in the hot sun with sweat dripping from him. Why?" No one could answer.

When the boy's grandfather died, trouble began. Nanaue longed for meat, but his uncles would not let him have it. "You must never taste this food," they told him. "Those were your father's words."

"But I have tasted meat," he said at last. "My grandfather gave it to me, saying it would make me strong and brave. I like it better than any other food and must have more."

Still the uncles refused. "You never should have tasted it," they said. But this refusal came too late. Harm was already done.

About this time strange accidents occurred which set neighbors questioning once more. Swimmers were drowned. Were they carried out by some current or devoured by a shark? No one could say. Every time this happened Nanaue had called a warning. "Where are you going?" he would shout to the young men on their way to the sea pool and would add, "Don't go today. The sea pool is not safe."

"Why?" the neighbors wondered. Did Nanaue know the danger? How did he know? Again, no one could answer.

One day the high chief's crier went about summoning men to work on 'Umi's farm. "Come tomorrow!" he said. "'Umi calls for all who are strong to come and work for him."

At dawn all started for the high chief's fields. Perhaps the work would be hard but it was fun to work, many together. A passing group of men called to Nanaue. "You cannot work in Kalei's field today," they said. "'Umi has called for all." But Nanaue went on working as if he had not heard them.

Soon someone went to the high chief. "Why is it Nanaue works at home?" he questioned. "Did you not summon all, O Heavenly One?" And 'Umi sent his guards for Nanaue.

The young man came and stood before the chief, looking fearlessly into 'Umi's eyes. "I did not understand I was to come," he said.

'Umi, pleased with the handsome youth of fearless bearing, spoke kindly. "All were called," he said. "You did not understand. Go now and work." So Nanaue went to work, wearing his *kīhei*.

"He did not understand!" one young man said to his companions and added scornfully, "I called to him myself. I know he heard."

"That is true," the others answered. "We told him 'Umi had called everyone."

"Look at him now!"

"He works well. See how he lifts the earth with his digging stick. He is both strong and quick."

"But he works alone, as always."

"And he wears a *kīhei!* Did anyone ever see him without the *kīhei?*"

"Let us pull it off," one young man said.

"How can we get near him? He keeps away from us."

"We should make him angry."

"We could make it seem an accident," the first man said. "I have a plan."

A little later one of these young men broke his digging stick and snatched the stick belonging to another. The second chased him. As the two ran behind Nanaue the second caught the *kīhei* and pulled it off. There was a shout and everybody turned to look. Nanaue's back was uncovered and on it a great shark's mouth was snapping at the two young men.

People cried out in wonder and in fear. Nanaue ran and a crowd followed him. Down to the beach he ran and stood for a moment poised upon the rocks. As the crowd came closer he leaped from them to the sea.

They reached the rocks and saw a great shark swimming and snapping its jaws at them. They saw it turn, shake its tail scornfully, then swim away.

The people were filled with anger. Now that Nanaue was gone their anger turned against his mother and his uncles. These were seized, bound and brought before the chief. Men told the story eagerly. "Nanaue is a shark! He had a great shark's mouth upon his back. It is he who has killed the swimmers. He is gone but since his family remain, let them be punished for the evil he has done."

'Umi quieted the people. "Let us hear what Kalei and her brothers have to say," he told them.

Trembling, Kalei told her story. She told of her marriage to the shark chief and of his words to her before he went away. "My son has never tasted meat," she said.

"Oh Kalei, he has," a brother answered sadly. "Our father fed it to the boy, saying the pork would make him strong and brave."

"He did it secretly," another added. "We did not know of this until our father died. Then Nanaue called for meat and we refused."

"And so he got his own!" 'Umi said sadly. "The old man should have obeyed the father's words. Now we must listen to the shark chief who is both wise and kind. He never lets his sharks harm people of Hawai'i. Kalei was his wife and we must not punish her against his will."

'Umi turned to his wise *kahuna*. "This family shall be kept in the prison house," he said. "Pray to the shark chief. If it be his will that they be punished, they shall be. If it be his will that they be set free, we shall obey him. And what of Nanaue? Will the shark chief promise that his son shall not harm people of Hawai'i? Pray for an answer to these words, O my *kahuna*.

The next day the *kahuna* brought an answer. "The shark chief has spoken," he said. "Last night, as I slept, I heard his voice speaking these words: 'May you live long, O 'Umi, high chief of Hawai'i. My son has done great wrong, but the first wrongdoing was his grandfather's. The old man should have obeyed my words. Therefore my son shall not be punished but I promise he shall never again come near this island of Hawai'i.'"

"And you, O 'Umi, must set free my wife. She and her brothers must not be punished for another's wrong. Let there be peace between us, sharks and men. This is my will."

"The shark chief's words shall be obeyed," 'Umi said at once. "Set free the prisoners. Wrong has been done but it was not their wrong. Let no one by cruelty to Kalei rouse the anger of the sharks."

The anger of the crowd had cooled and people understood that unkindness toward his wife might cause the shark chief to do them harm. So she and her brothers were treated kindly. And Nanaue never again harmed people on his island.

From Hawaiian Folk Tales *by Thrum.*

The Shark That Came for *Poi*

"See that shark!"

"He is a big one! What do you suppose he wants?"

As the men paddled toward the Kona coast they watched the great shark following their canoe. "What do you want, old shark?" one asked at last. "Do you know that we carry *pa'i'ai* to Kona to our relatives? Do you eat *poi*, O shark? Here then!" and the man threw a small bundle toward the shark.

The great fish did not catch and swallow the food but pushed it with his nose. The men saw him swimming toward shore, pushing the little bundle through the waves. They watched him as long as he was in sight. "That is a strange thing," 'Aukai said. "He seemed to know we had a load of *pa'i'ai*."

"But he did not eat it," another answered. "Who ever saw a shark pushing food through the waves as that one did?"

"And why did he want it?" 'Aukai asked again. "Where was he taking it?"

The next week these men again paddled from Kohala to Kona with *pa'i'ai*, the dry, pounded *kalo* from which *poi* is made. Again the shark followed and again swam toward the shore pushing before him the small bundle thrown to him. This happened many times.

Then one day 'Aukai said, "I mean to find out about that shark. You paddle toward Kona with the food and throw a bundle to the shark as you always do. I shall follow in a small canoe and see if I can learn what the shark does with the bundle."

'Aukai's canoe was some distance behind the larger one. He saw the men throw the bundle of food and watched the shark swim with it to a Kona beach. Then a

strange thing happened. ‘Aukai saw an old man come down the beach, leaning on a stick. ‘Aukai watched as the old man picked up the bundle and hobbled to his house.

Very curious, the Kohala man beached his canoe beyond a point of land and walked along the shore. He came to the house the old man had entered. "O friend!" he called, "here is a thirsty one. Can you give me a drink?"

The old man hobbled to the door. "You are welcome, stranger," he said. "Come in, drink and eat. Our water is a bit brackish but it will cure your thirst." He brought a gourd of water. Then he brought out fish and *poi.* "Eat," he repeated.

‘Aukai took the food. He had looked quickly about the little place and noticed that only the man and his wife lived there. Still he wondered. "This food tastes good to a hungry traveler," he said. "I thank you, old man. But I wonder at the *poi.* Can one so old as you work in the *kalo* patch?"

"Alas no," the old man answered, "and we have no relative in this village to bring food. But in the bay we have a friend. A good shark brings us fish. Of late he brings *poi* too. Every few days he comes with a bundle of *pa‘i‘ai* for us. I pound it with fresh water and make the good *poi* which you taste."

"Where does the shark get the *pa‘i‘ai?*" ‘Aukai asked, wondering whether the man knew.

The old man answered simply, "The gods provide."

‘Aukai paddled back to his Kohala village and told what he had seen and heard. The people were full of wonder and sympathy. "The poor old folks," they said, "with no child to care for them!" And, "What a wise shark! After this he shall have a big bundle of food each week."

And so he did. For many months the shark was given a big bundle of *pa‘i‘ai* whenever the canoe went to Kona, and the bundle was dropped for him close to the beach where the old couple lived.

Then one day the shark did not come. The next week, still, he was not seen. "I shall take the food," 'Aukai said, and paddled straight to the old man's village. He found the little home empty. Not even mats or bowls were there. Aukai went to a neighbor. "I have come to see the old man who used to live in that house," he told him, pointing.

"He is dead," the neighbor answered, "and his wife has gone to relatives in another village."

'Aukai paddled back to Kohala and told his friends. "The shark's work is done," he said. The shark was never seen again.

Told by Mary Kawena Pūku'i.

Punia and the Sharks

"**P**unia, my son, you must be content to care for our garden and to dive for fish in mountain pools."

"But, Mother, I long for lobster such as we used to have. I long to dive for them."

"You know quite well, Punia, why no one in Kohala has such food today. Since the coming of those evil sharks our waters are not safe. Too many lives have been lost to those man-eaters. Shellfish and crabs are good with our sweet potatoes. Say no more of diving."

Punia obeyed his mother's command but, under his breath, he muttered, "When I am a man I shall make an end of those man-eaters!"

Years passed but Punia did not forget the promise he had made. "Mother," he said one day, "I go to dive for lobsters."

"No, no!" she answered. "You must not go to the lobster pit. Always the evil sharks watch that place, lurking in the shadows. You shall not go."

"I am a man," Punia told her firmly, "and a man decides such matters for himself. I shall be very careful but I go to dive for lobsters."

Hina knew she could no longer hold him back and prayed the gods to give him wisdom and protection.

Punia also prayed. Then he went out to the bay where the man-eating sharks made their home. There too was the lobster pit. There must be many lobsters, for years had passed since the fishermen of Kohala had dared to use the pool. Nearby in the shadow of the rocky point the young man saw the sharks, eleven of them. A chief man-eater, Kaiʻaleʻale, and his ten followers had come to make their home and cause fear along the Kohala coast.

Long Punia stood and watched those sharks sleeping in the shadow. Then he lifted his voice and called as if to some companions, "The sharks are sleeping here, and I shall dive out in the sea for lobsters." The next moment he threw a great stone far out. The sharks were after it at once, swimming threateningly about the place where the stone had sunk and looking for the one whose voice they heard.

Meanwhile Punia dived into the unguarded pit, secured two lobsters and was back on the rocks while the sharks still hunted around the stone. "O Kai‘ale‘ale!" he shouted tauntingly, "I got my lobsters in spite of two sharks, ten sharks, twenty sharks! It was the one with the thin tail who helped me." And he stood watching while the ten fell upon the thin-tailed shark and killed him.

"That is one," he said with satisfaction. "They are stupid as well as cruel, those man-eaters, not like the wise, kind sharks who are our guardians and friends." To his mother he said, "We have lobsters to eat with our sweet potatoes today," and Hina rejoiced at her son's safe return.

After a time he went to her again. "I go to dive for lobsters," he told her. "It is no use to try to dissuade me, Mother. Those sharks are stupid and I can outwit them."

Again he stood on the rocky point and called as if to friends, "The sharks sleep near the lobster pit and I shall not dive here today. One the other side is a place my mother told me of. It is safe to dive there." He ran across the point of land, threw a stone into deep water, ran back and dived into the lobster pit. The sharks were still swimming around the place where the stone had sunk when Punia returned to the rocks. "O Kai‘ale‘ale!" he shouted, "I dived swiftly and got my lobsters with the help of the fat-stomached shark!"

"Why did you help Punia?" shouted the shark chief to the one with the fat stomach. "You shall die!"

And the young man saw those cruel sharks kill another of their company. "That is two," he said as he went home.

Time after time the same trick was played until a day came when the young man could say, "That is ten!" The chief, Kai'ale'ale, alone remained. He was one only, but huge and fierce. To battle with him would mean death for any man. Another trick was needed.

"Mother," Punia said one day, "can you make me a mat? I want it small and very closely plaited." She made the mat and Punia got two sticks and a bundle of food.

"O Hina," he said to his mother. "I am going on a journey. I may be gone for many days. Do not be anxious for me but pray the gods to give me safe return." He took her in his arms, then hurried off, carrying mat, sticks, and food.

Once more he stood on the point of land and saw where the great shark chief slept in the shadow. "Do you sleep, Kai'ale'ale?" he shouted. "Waken and hear my words! Your followers are dead. Now Punia comes to fight with you. Fight with all your power but remember this! If you kill me my mother can bring me back to life and you will surely perish. Only do not swallow me, for I should die and she could not revive me. O man-eating Chief, I dive! I dive!"

Down he went close to the shark who opened his huge mouth to swallow his enemy. Punia entered, unscratched. As he went through the mouth he stopped to wedge in his sticks so that the great jaws could not close, then fastened the mat in the shark's throat to keep out water. Once inside the great fish, Punia did all he could to give him pain.

With jaws propped wide and great pain in his stomach, Kai'ale'ale sought for help. Other sharks saw him. "O Kai'ale'ale," they shouted, "why do you fly so swiftly through the waves? Is some enemy following you?"

"It is the son of Hina who is hurting my insides!" the shark chief answered. "I am rushing to find help."

He rushed here and there but found no help. On he rushed for many days till Punia lost track of time and distance and knew not where he was. He did all he could to hurt the shark but he, also, was being hurt, for the rough stomach of the fish had made him sore and rubbed off all his hair till he was bald. I must make end of this! the young man told himself.

He heard the break of waves on reef. Some land is here, he thought, and any land is better than this stomach!

"O Kai'ale'ale," he shouted through the open mouth, "I have brought evil to you as I promised. Now let me out. I shall remove the sticks and shall injure you no more. Only let me out upon the outer reef. Do not take me to the beach where strangers may find and kill me."

Stupid still, the shark chief swam across the reef, eager to bring death to his enemy. He stranded himself on the beach as the young man had planned. Punia was about to crawl out when he heard voices. "A shark! Here is a stranded shark! Let us kill him!" Soon people were raining blows on the helpless fish.

"O Kai'ale'ale," Punia shouted, "here you perish! I promised that you and your followers should die. My promise is fulfilled."

The shark rolled over and over trying to kill the enemy inside him but he himself was gasping and his struggles and the blows of men ended his life.

Punia heard the blows and saw sharp knives piercing the stomach. "Oh, be careful," he shouted, "lest you cut the man inside."

"What was that?" he heard one ask.

"Nothing!" the others answered.

The first man told them, "I heard a faint voice calling, 'Be careful lest you cut the man inside!' There is an evil spirit in this shark. Let it alone."

"Nonsense! There was no voice. Shark meat is food for our chief. The flesh of this brave fish will give him courage. We heard no voice but run away if you are fearful!" and the men went to work once more.

Then Punia shouted with all his strength, "Oh, be careful lest you hurt the man inside!" The pounding and cutting stopped and the young man heard frightened cries as the people rushed away.

Now was the moment for escape! He removed the mat but, as he looked through the open jaws, Punia saw more people coming with knives and adzes. He drew back and covered himself with the mat, for he knew not where he was and feared the people of this island would kill a bald-headed man when they saw him crawl out of the shark. As they went to work cutting the great fish Punia shouted again and frightened them away.

This happened several times but always more people came. If only he could reach the woods unseen!

Darkness at last! The young man peeped out. The beach was filled with people curious yet afraid. He saw how they watched the shark while a few stole fearfully toward it. Perhaps he could frighten them away.

Punia crawled through the jaws and ran to the forest. All about he heard terrified cries and people ran wildly from him. "An evil spirit!" they were shouting. "A bald-headed spirit!"

Punia was safe in the forest. No one was near. But where was he? Must he live long on some strange island? And what of his poor mother who would think him dead?

Walking steadily and quietly he made his way until he reached an open place. He looked about and drew a breath of wonder and relief, for before him in the moonlight Mauna Kea rose! The shark had returned to Hawai'i!

Punia traveled steadily until he reached his home. All Kohala rejoiced that the man-eaters were dead and the lobster pool was theirs to use once more.

As told by Westervelt in T.K.K. Topics, *Apr. 1914*
(Mission Houses Museum Library).

The Kihapū

In the days when Kiha was chief of Waipi'o life in that valley was made miserable by the sounding of the *menehune pū*. Above the cliff-walled valley was *menhune* land where the little people lived their lives with small concern for the Hawaiians below. Our night was day for them and it was then they blew upon their *pū*, or conch-shell trumpet. Down into the valley came the clear sound of the *pū* to be tossed back and forth by echoing cliffs till all Waipi'o was filled with sound. Dogs woke and barked, babies cried and there was little sleep to be had the whole night through.

Kiha, the chief, offered a reward to any man who would steal the *pū* and bring it to him. But no tall Hawaiian could go unnoticed into *menehune* land. Such an attempt was useless!

After a night of noise and sleeplessness morning was still. Kiha settled himself for a much-needed sleep. Suddenly two guards appeared. "O Heavenly One," they said, "come out and see our prisoners."

Angrily the chief left his mats and stumbled to the *heiau*. He was in no mood to listen patiently. The guards led before him an old man with arms tightly bound. Close behind the man followed a large yellow dog.

"Speak!" the chief commanded his guards, though he was ready to condemn those who disturbed his rest, caring little for the crime.

"Long life, O Heavenly One!" said a guard. "Someone was digging in your *'awa* patch. For days we have seen loose earth where the *'awa* roots were pulled. Last night we hid and watched. O Heavenly One, we saw this dog dig up your *'awa* and walk away carrying the good roots in his mouth. We followed it to the mountain home of this old man. He has trained the beast to steal our good chief's *'awa.*"

"Let them die, both dog and man!" said the chief impatiently.

"O Heavenly One, will you not hear the old man?" The voice of the *kahuna* was quiet but Kiha knew his wisdom and his power.

"Very well," he answered. "Speak, old man."

"O Heavenly One!" The old man's voice was trembling. "I did not know my dog took *'awa* from your garden. He did not know. O Heavenly One, I pray you spare my dog. He meant no wrong."

"You pray for his life and not your own?" Kiha asked curiously.

"O Heavenly One, he is my child and I am old," the man replied. "My wife and I were childless. We found a pup, a little yellow pup with friendly, playful ways. We fed and cared for him. He became a son to us. Now we are old, he cares for us as a loving son cares for old parents."

The man's eyes shone with love and his voice was stronger. "He saw I wanted *'awa* and brought it to me. I thought he brought wild roots from the forest. O Heavenly One, I am sure the dog did not know the *'awa* patch was yours."

"I have listened to your words," Kiha said, still anxious to get back to his sleeping mats. "You had no right to steal my *'awa.* You both shall die!"

"Long life, O Heavenly One!" The *kahuna* had been looking keenly at the dog. "This is no common beast. I see great wisdom in his eyes. Do him no harm."

For the first time the chief looked carefully at the dog. The animal's eyes looked at him fearlessly and, yes, they were wise eyes! A sudden thought came to Kiha. "Do you think," he asked the old man, "that your dog could get something for me? Each night the *menehune* blow their conch-shell trumpet. There is no sleep for me! No sleep for all Waipi'o! Do you think your dog can get that *pū*?"

"I do not know," the old man answered and turned to the dog. "Do you think you can get the *pū*?" he asked. The dog gave his master a quick look of understanding and wagged his tail. "He will try," the man said simply.

Kiha was no longer sleepy. "Take the man to the prison house," he commanded, "but set free the dog. If the animal brings the *pū*, his master also shall be free."

Puapua, the yellow dog, licked his master's hand as if to say, "I shall free you," swam the Waipi'o River and disappeared up the trail.

As he climbed he changed his form and became smaller. When he trotted into the *menehune* village he was just such a puppy as he had been when his master first found him. With a coconut husk in his mouth he frolicked up to the first *menehune* he met, asking him to play.

The *menehune* are friendly and frolicsome, and in a very short time several were playing with the cunning pup, chasing him, pulling his coconut husk away from him, running and inviting him to chase.

This way and that dashed the puppy. He would pause for breath in the doorway of some house, then dash madly off again. Soon all the villagers were joining the fun. Back and forth through the village darted the pup, running swiftly and now and then stopping to peek into a house. At last he found what he was looking for—the *pū*, hanging by a cord not far from the door of a dark house.

Still Puapua played, the cunningest, most frolicsome little pup the *menehune* had ever seen. They loved his puppy ways and hoped to keep him. When, tired out, the little men sank down to sleep, the puppy too lay down, rested his head on his paws and slept—or seemed to sleep.

Opening one eye, Puapua saw that two or three *menhune* were still awake and closed his eye again. The village was very quiet. There was no sound except the soft breathing of the little men. Puapua opened his eyes once more and stretched his legs. Everyone seemed to be asleep. Slowly he rose and looked about then quietly made his way to the house where he had seen the *pū*.

It was a big yellow dog who loosened the conch-shell trumpet, got it firmly in his mouth and stole out of the village onto the trail. Then he ran! But, as he ran swiftly, the wind blew through the conch with a low whistling. That sound woke the *menehune.* Their *pū!* Their *pū* was gone! In a moment they were following the sound.

Puapua heard them coming and took a short cut. The shell struck a rock and gave forth a resounding blast. A bit had been broken off but the dog did not stop. His pursuers were close now. He reached the river, leaped in and swam across.

But the *menehune* stopped. Dawn was close. Before daylight every *menehune* must be at home. Sadly they returned without their *pū.*

Kiha and the *kahuna* had been waiting. They heard faintly the blast from the *pū* as it struck the rock. What did that mean? Suddenly, right before them, the big dog scrambled from the river and dropped the *pū* at Kiha's feet. Eagerly the chief picked it up. He had it! No more sleepless nights!

"Take the ropes from the prisoner," he commanded the guards. "Set him free."

"Old man," he said when the prisoner came before him, "you dog has done great service. The corner of my *'awa* patch where he dug, that shall be yours as long as you live. The dog shall dig from that corner all the *'awa* that his master needs. May you live long—you and your wife and dog."

Kiha kept the *pū*. With it he sent messages or summoned workers. From that time it bore his name—

the Kihapū. Next time you go to Bishop Museum look at the conch-shell trumpets in Hawaiian Hall. You'll see where a bit has been broken from one of them. Some say that is the Kihapū.

Told by Mary Kawena Pūkuʻi.

The Cowry Shell

Puakō stood on the beach with a bit of seaweed in her hand. As she tossed it into the waves for an offering she prayed to the fish god,

"O Kū'ula,
Keep me safe from harm from the sea,
Safe from all evil."

Wading out a few steps she gathered another bit of seaweed and prayed again,

"O Hina,
Keep me safe from harm from the land,
Safe from all evil."

She threw this seaweed toward the land.

After her prayers her work began. She gathered a few shellfish then waded along the coral to a clump of seaweed she had seen. I must fill my gourd, she thought. We must have food!

Alas! I wish my husband could make a better living. Some fishermen bring home a load of fish but Kainoa is gone all day and gets only three or four *he'e*. Perhaps he does not work hard, perhaps he does not pray enough or perhaps he is just unlucky. I don't know. But I wish he had *he'e* enough to trade for all things that we need: for mats, bowls and vegetable food, for all the things that other people have, and Puakō sighed longingly.

Farther out she saw another clump of seaweed and waded toward it. In a deep pool something caught her eye. Was that a *he'e* half hidden by a rock? It was! A big one! If only she had a spear! Looking about, she saw a pointed stick on the beach. She waded toward it quietly and a moment later thrust its point into the *heʻe*. How the animal clung to its rock! If only Kainoa were here he would know just how to get it loose. Puakō tried a sideways jerk. At last she had it. She bit between the eyes till the animal was limp then left it on a dry rock well above the reach of waves.

Hardly thinking what she did, she waded back to that same pool and looked below the rock. There, in the very same place, was another *heʻe!* Down went the pointed stick. With a quick jerk she brought up the animal, bit it and laid it by the first.

Straight back to the pool she waded but could hardly believe her eyes. There, in the same place, was a third! This went on until Puakō had all the *heʻe* she could carry. Then she hurried home. Won't my husband be surprised! That was all she could think of as she scrambled over rocks and crossed moist sand.

There was Kainoa sitting on the beach, his head between his knees. How tired and discouraged he looked! And how surprised and glad he would be in a moment. Puakō did not speak until she stood before her husband. Then she said, "Kainoa!"

He looked up startled, then sprang to his fee. *"Heʻe!"* he exclaimed. "Who gave them to you?"

"No one! I caught them."

"You could not—not all those!"

"Put them in a safe place," she said, "and come with me. I shall show you."

Puakō led her husband to the beach where she had been gathering shellfish. They waded quietly to her pool and she pointed.

"A *heʻe!*" Kainoa whispered and down went his spear. A moment later he was carrying his catch to the dry rock. "Let us go home," he said. "I will salt two and trade the rest for chickens, *kalo* and bananas. Tonight we shall feast!"

But Puakō stood still beside the pool and beckoned. When Kainoa came to her she pointed. "Another!" In a moment he had that also.

"But why do they come here?" he wondered after he had caught four. He bent over the pool, searching the rocks with his eyes. "That red cowry shell!" he whispered and stooped to pull it loose from its crack in the rock. "This is a cowry loved by the *he'e*. With this I shall be a lucky fisherman. You shall see!"

Next day Kainoa fastened the cowry to a line and used it as bait. He caught two *he'e* but one let go the cowry and was lost. "I need a hook," the fisherman said. He firmly tied a bone hook below the cowry shell and added a small heavy stone as sinker. He paddled to deeper water and dropped his cowry bait. He waited only a moment until he felt something on his line. A *he'e!* The cowry had, indeed, brought luck.

And the luck held. Day after day Kainoa caught all the *he'e* that he needed, both for food and trade. Part of each day he fished for *he'e* and part of each day he worked in his sweet potato garden or cooked or feasted with his friends. He had become an important man because of that cowry shell.

Now word of that wonderful shell went about Kohala and came even to the ears of a chief living in Kona. This chief also was a fisherman. He loved *he'e* and desired the shell. He called a trusted servant. "Go to Kohala," the chief commanded. "Find a man called Kainoa and see if these rumors of a lucky cowry shell are true. If they are true then steal the shell for me."

Some days later the servant returned. "The rumors are true," he told the chief. "I have watched Kainoa fish. He has only to drop his shell over the canoe side. In a moment he pulls it up with a fine *he'e* coiled around it. It is a beautiful shell, deep red, a color these animals love."

"Where is it?" asked the chief. "I commanded you to bring it to me."

"O Heavenly One, Kainoa loves that shell as he loves life itself. He never leaves it in the gourd with his fish-hooks but keeps it in a safe fold of his *malo*. Even in his sleep he holds the cowry in his hand. It is impossible to steal it from him."

"That we shall see," was the answer of the chief. He called another servant, a sly and clever man and a swift runner. "Go," he said, "to Kohala and find a fisherman named Kainoa. Stay with him, work for him, make your-self his trusted friend. Stay a year if need be but steal for me his lucky cowry shell—the beautiful red shell he uses to catch *heʻe*. Bring that to me and you shall be rewarded."

A few days after this a stranger came to Kainoa's home. He was a wandering fellow but good-natured, a clever storyteller and a good companion. Kainoa gave him food, for he liked the fellow's talk. Next day he found the man a willing worker. Kainoa had food enough for an extra mouth and let the man stay on to work in the sweet potato patch or paddle the canoe. Kainoa and Puakō became fond of the young man. He was like a younger brother and always ready for work or fun. He stayed with them nearly a year.

Then one day he became very sick. He lay upon his mats and did not eat. Kainoa prepared good food and brought it to the young man, but the sick one weakly refused. "Let me alone, my friend," he whispered. "Let me die."

Kainoa went out alone to work in his potato patch. His heart was heavy for he loved the young man. The sun grew warm and Kainoa stopped to rest. Suddenly he thought of his cowry shell. I did not bring it with me! he said to himself. I was thinking of my friend and did not slip the shell inside my *malo*. I must go for it or some neighbor's prying eyes may find it. Many want that lucky cowry.

He hurried to the sleeping house. The sick man was gone from his mats and Kainoa could not find the cowry shell. He looked quickly in the house where fishing things were kept and then knew what had happened. His fishhook gourd was on the floor. Beside it lay a tangled line and sinker. He must have left the cowry there last night. The man he called his friend had seen and stolen it!

Kainoa climbed up a long trail which ran behind his house. In the distance he saw a man and started after him. But the man saw Kainoa, went faster and disappeared in the direction of Kona. It was a trick! Kainoa told himself bitterly. He was no friend but one who came to trick me!

Kainoa's only thought was to find his cowry. He went to a wise *kahuna* but the *kahuna* did not know how to help him. For many days the fisherman wandered, thinking bitter thoughts and asking help, but finding none.

At last he found one that could help him. "It is a chief who has your cowry," this *kahuna* said, "the chief who lives on the Kona coast."

"A chief!" repeated Kainoa. "He sent that man to trick me. How can I ever get my cowry from a chief?"

The *kahuna* sat long thinking. "I'll tell you, Kainoa," he said at last. "On O'ahu lives a clever boy called 'Iwa. He is still a child, but the day will come when he will be the cleverest trickster in all our islands. Even now he knows juggling tricks and he is sly. Go to this 'Iwa, treat him as if he were a man rather than a child and tell him of your trouble. It may be he can get your cowry back."

So Kainoa went to 'Iwa. The boy was pleased to have a man in trouble come to him for help and listened thoughtfully. At last he said, "Return to your home, O Kainoa. In a few days I shall paddle to the Kona coast and

find that chief. I shall bring back your cowry shell to you."
Kainoa paddled back to Kohala wondering. This ʻIwa was
only a boy. How could he get the cowry?

ʻIwa made ready for a voyage and paddled to
Hawaiʻi. He went along the Kona coast, stopping now and
then to eat and chat. He heard where the chief was living
and went to his landing place.

On the beach in front of the chief's house he found
two young girls busy with a game. He stopped and chat-
ted with them. He told them riddles and amused them
with his juggling tricks. The girls liked the boy and told
him they were daughters of the chief. "Where is your
father?" ʻIwa asked carelessly.

"Out fishing. He has a new cowry shell, a red shell
that is loved by *heʻe*. He goes fishing with it every day.
A little while ago we saw him paddle out." They pointed
the direction.

ʻIwa stayed a little longer, laughing and chatting with
the girls. Then he said that he also was a fisherman and
must get back to work. He found an old man to do the
paddling while he fished. But ʻIwa had no luck that day.
"I do not know these fishing grounds," he said as he
moved the canoe from place to place.

At last he came near another canoe—a red one. That
was the chief's canoe. There was the chief fishing with
Kainoa's cowry!

A few moments later ʻIwa said to his companion, "My
hook is caught on coral. I cannot pull it up. Hold the
canoe in this place while I get it loose." He slid quietly
over the side and swam under water to the chief's line.
Working carefully he took Kainoa's red cowry from the
chief's line and tied a common cowry shell in its place.
Then he swam back to his own canoe. "I got my hook
free," he said as he pulled it up, "but I have caught nothing and am going home."

The next day Kainoa had his own dearly loved cowry shell. Never again did luck leave him. He and Puakō had all things that they needed. 'Iwa returned to O'ahu with a good reward. He spent his life in tricks and thieving and some of his thieving was not so honest as when he stole the cowry shell for its rightful owner. Men of Hawai'i still catch *he'e* with a red cowry tied to hook and sinker as Kainoa taught them.

From "The Story of a Cowry" by Emerson in
Mid-Pacific Magazine, *Mar. 1920.*

Food for Kohala

"**H**arken, you fishermen, why don't you pull in your net?" Pūpū had noticed two fishermen with their net in the water. Curious as to what they were catching, he had paddled near and spat out the juice of the *kukui* nut he had been chewing. The oil of the nut spread over the water, quieting its ripples. Now Pūpū could plainly see the net under water. It was full of fish.

"Why don't you pull in your net?" he asked again. "It is full of fish."

"Go away!" one of the fishermen said crossly. "There are no fish in our net and there never will be if you stay here talking. Go away!"

"But I tell you it is full of fish!" Pūpū said again. "I can see them. Can't you?"

The two fishermen were looking into the water. They too were chewing something and spitting out juice to quiet ripples. Why didn't they see the fish?

"Let us pull in the net," the second man said. "We have been here a long time. If we get no fish, we can paddle to another spot."

So they pulled in the net and Pūpū listened to their words of surprise and joy when they found it was, indeed, full. "How did you know?" the second fisherman asked Pūpū.

"This *kukui* oil," Pūpū told him. "I chew the nut and spit it out. The oil quiets the water. What were you chewing?"

"Sea beans. Let us try this wonderful nut."

Pūpū handed them two nuts. Each man chewed and spat out the oil. They watched as it spread, quieting the ripples. "Look!" they cried in great surprise. "You can see the coral!"

"See that little striped fish swimming about! This is a door to the underwater world. It is indeed a wonderful nut. Have you more, stranger? It would be good to plant these nuts so that we could have many to use."

Pūpū gave the fishermen all the nuts he had with him. "I can get more," he said.

They, in turn, gave him food—*kalo* and sweet potatoes wrapped in *kī* leaves. Pūpū tasted. "I never ate such food!" he said and put the rest into a gourd bowl.

"Why don't you eat it?" one man asked.

"I am going to take it home to plant," Pūpū told him. "We have nothing so good as this in Kohala."

The men laughed. "You can't plant this!" they said. "It has been cooked."

Pūpū's face was full of disappointment. The men watched him and one said, "Maybe I can help you get some vegetables for planting."

"Are there plenty where you live?" asked Pūpū.

"There is a land not far away where some strange spirits live. They have all kinds of growing plants but they are evil spirits and will not share their food. We fish for these evil spirits and they pay us with cooked food. They never give us anything that we can plant."

"Then I can't get any," Pūpū said sadly.

"If you could make them think you were a spirit like them they would give you what you ask."

"But how can I do that?"

"I have a plan," the fisherman told him. "Go home and make a basket of 'ie'ie rootlets. Make a big one, big enough for me to hide in, and it must have a cover. Meet me tomorrow by that point of rock."

Wondering, Pūpū went back to Kohala. All the afternoon he worked, gathering roots and plaiting them into a basket. That is big enough to hold a man, he thought. But why does the fisherman want to get into a basket?

The next day he met the fisherman who explained his plan. "You see, these evil spirits would recognize me. They know that I am a man, their fisherman. But I will hide in the basket. You paddle to their shore and tell them you have come from down the coast for vegetables for planting. Tell them you are a spirit of their land. They will try you to see whether you know their way and I will whisper what you must say or do. Don't let them find me or there will be trouble for us both."

The fisherman got into the basket in the stern of Pūpū's canoe and Pūpū covered him. Then he paddled boldly toward the land of evil spirits.

The spirit guards hailed him: "Who are you and why do you come?"

"I am a native of your land," Pūpū answered. "I come from farther down the coast. The spirits of my district sent me to get vegetables for planting. Give me safe landing."

"Give him safe landing!" a guard commanded, and at his words, the surf was quiet in one spot.

Pūpū would have paddled to that spot, but the hidden fisherman whispered a warning: "That is not the landing place. He has quieted the surf at the place where they dump refuse. Ask again."

Pūpū shouted to the guards, "Do you expect a native son to land on the refuse pile? Give me quiet landing at the landing beach."

Again the guard shouted a command and the surf was quieted beside a sandy beach. "That is right," the fisherman whispered and Pūpū paddled to the shore.

The spirits crowded around to look at him. They seemed like men but there was a strange look in their eyes. One offered to help Pūpū beach his canoe.

Pūpū thanked him. "You lift the bow," he said. "I myself will carry the stern for it is *kapu*—only I may lift it."

He said this because he did not want the spirit to know he had a heavy man in the basket.

Because he had asked for the right landing place the spirits thought Pūpū must be a spirit like themselves. Still they were not sure. "Let us see if he knows our vegetables," they whispered to each other.

So vegetables were brought to the canoe. "Here is food," a spirit said and offered Pūpū something he had never seen.

"No," whispered the voice from the basket. "That is food eaten only a famine time. Do not take it."

"I did not come for famine food!" Pūpū told the spirits. "Give me good vegetables for planting."

The spirit held out something else. "That is a yam," whispered the voice. "It is good food."

Pūpū held out his hand saying:

"I take this yam
May it grow well.
We shall bake it
And our wives and children
Shall be fed."

"This stranger is indeed one of us," the spirits said. "He knows our vegetables." They went on offering Pūpū different kinds of *kalo,* sweet potatoes and other vegetables. Always he obeyed the whispered voice and chose the best. Satisfied, the spirits helped him launch his canoe and watched him paddle down the coast.

When the canoe was hidden from the spirit land Pūpū helped the fisherman out of the basket and they paddled home. They divided the good vegetables between them.

That is the way that *kalo* and sweet potatoes came to the people of Kohala.

From Hawaiian Antiquities and Folklore *by Fornander.*

The Land Beneath The Sea

There is a land beneath the sea where people live as we do. There are villages where people work and swim, wrestle and box just as those do who live above upon the earth. In that land lived a certain chief who had many children but only one beloved daughter. Because of his great love for this girl, Hina, the chief wanted special care for her. "Servants are not enough," he said, and ordered Kīpapa, her young brother, to be always with Hina whenever she left home.

Kīpapa loved his sister dearly and was faithful to his trust until a certain day. On this day he was rolling the *maika* stone with other men when a servant came to him. "O Heavenly One," the servant said, "Hina has sent for you. She is going surfing with her women and asks you to join them."

"Don't go!" the young men cried. "It will spoil the game. You are winning. Do not go!"

Kīpapa hesitated. His father had commanded that he be always with Hina when she left her home and yet— She has many servants, the young man thought. Surely she is safe. He turned to the one who had brought the message. "Tell my sister I shall come soon. I shall come when the *maika* game is ended," and he went on playing.

That morning the chief stood watching the girls surf. Hina came riding a wave. How beautiful she was, his precious child! He looked about for her brother. Where was Kīpapa? The chief's anger blazed as he went to look for his son.

He heard shouting. Was that boy taking part in some game instead of guarding Hina? In a moment the chief came upon the men at the *maika* course. "Disobedient boy!" he shouted. "So this is the way you obey my command while evil threatens Hina!"

"What evil threatens?" Kīpapa asked. "Surely the servants—"

"Servants! I commanded you to guard her. Disobedient one!"

"But, Father, I have been faithful to my trust. Always—"

"Silence!" shouted the angry chief. "I care not for the past. Today you disobey me. Leave my sight. Leave this land. Let me never look upon your face again."

Kīpapa walked away with slow steps and hanging head. He had been disobedient, it was true, but only once. And for one hour of carelessness he must leave the sister whom he loved, his companions and all the life he knew. Where could he go?

Sorely troubled, the boy came to the home of his grandfather. "My father is angry with me," he told the old man. "He has sent me away and I have nowhere to go." The grandfather looked long at the strong, clear-eyed lad. "Grandson," he said, "above us is another land—a land of sunlight, a land of work and games much like our own. Go there. Make for yourself a good life in that land."

Kīpapa's eyes were shining now with hope. "How?" he asked. "How can I go?"

"I shall open a way for you," the old man answered, "but say good-by to Hina for she loves you well."

So Kīpapa went to her saying, "Our father has sent me away, my sister. He says I am unfaithful to my trust."

Hina's face was full of sorrow. "Where can you go, my brother? Oh where in this world can you go?"

"To the land above, to the great land of sunlight. Even now our grandfather is opening a way for me."

"Then I shall go with you," whispered the girl. "You are my dearest friend! I shall go with you."

Kīpapa hesitated. It would be good to have a companion on this adventure but there might be danger and Hina was a woman. "Wait!" he said. "If I find that land is good I will come for you. I must go at once. If Father knew I talked with you his anger would blaze again. Farewell! In this bowl of coconut is my dearest treasure. I am giving it to you. Farewell, Hina, my sister."

He was gone, leaving in her hands a small bowl of polished coconut with a tight-fitting cover. Hina peeped inside. A treasure! A treasure that shone with clear light such as she had never seen. Carefully she put the bowl on a high shelf where no harm could reach it.

Kīpapa said farewell to his grandfather and went by the way that his grandfather had made, a crack in the ocean floor. Up through the water Kīpapa rose and looked about. Sunlight! Gleaming clouds! The great stretch of the sea, on and on to where the sky rested upon it. Wonderful! The young man gazed on this bright world, then noticed land and swam toward it.

It was a long swim and the sun had set before he reached the island. Land and sea were lighted only by the stars for, at that time, no moon had ever risen in the sky. Since rain was falling, Kīpapa sought shelter under an overturned canoe and fell asleep.

He was awakened by a hand upon his shoulder. Day had come. A man was bending over him saying, "Come with me to our chief. He has heard that you are here and bids you come to him."

Kīpapa rose and went before the chief, who gave him kindly greeting and welcomed him to his household. As the days passed this chief, Konikonia, came to love the young man almost as a son.

Kīpapa was very happy in his new life. He loved its work and sports and made many friends. Above all, he loved the light and warmth of sunshine. This land was good and his old home became only a dim memory. Even the thought of Hina became dim. He thought, instead, of the kindness of the chief and longed to repay that kindness. In all ways he was faithful to Konikonia, for Kīpapa loved him as if he were his father and longed to do some great deed for him. At last he found a way!

One day, as the two sat in the shade playing *kōnane,* the chief's fishermen approached. They stood waiting until the chief beckoned them near. He saw trouble in their faces and questioned them. One came forward to show a fishing line. "Look, O Heavenly one!" he said. "I dropped this line. Though I waited long, I felt no tiny trembling of the line as when a fish is hooked. At last I pulled it up. See! Every hook is gone! Not torn off, but neatly cut as with sharp stones. It is as if some man stood on the ocean floor and cut the line."

"My hooks are also gone!" another said.

"And mine!"

"Where were you fishing?" asked the chief. The men pointed. "It is strange—" the chief began.

Kīpapa jumped to his feet. "O Heavenly One," he said, "I know! At that place is a village of the Land Beneath the Sea. Someone from that village cut off the hooks!"

Konikonia looked keenly at him. Often he had wondered whence this young man had come. "Was that your village?" he questioned.

"Yes. Shall I go there and tell men not to cut your fishing lines?"

But the chief was thinking of something else. "There must be women in that Land Beneath the Sea." He spoke dreamily. Konikonia had no wife. "Tell me, Kīpapa, are they beautiful, the women of that land? Are they of chiefly family?"

The young man thought now of Hina, his sister, of her beauty and her longing to see the sunlit world above.

"O Heavenly One," he said, "I have a sister, a young chiefess, perfect in loveliness."

"Then bring her here, this lovely sister," the chief commanded.

Kīpapa chose his time with care, for his father must not know of his return. Down through the ocean he dropped, found the crack, and was once more in his own land. It was night but a gleam of light led him to Hina's home—a gleam of light that came from the bowl he had given her.

"Hina!" he whispered through the thatch. She woke. "Who calls?" Her answer was like the murmur of the wind.

"It is Kīpapa. I have come for you." In a moment Hina was at his side. "The coconut bowl," he whispered. "You must bring the treasure."

"I dare not wake my women," she replied. "I shall leave the bowl. If I like your sunlit land I'll send a servant to bring the treasure. Let us go."

Next morning Kīpapa led his sister before his well-loved chief. Konikonia looked upon her beauty and love woke in his heart. There was answering love in her dark eyes for the one who had shown kindness to her brother. So those two were married and Hina stayed in the land of sunlight.

"The treasure," she said one day to Kīpapa. "I must send for the coconut bowl."

He called a servant. "Go," they told the boy, giving directions. "The house stands by itself. Steal softly in and get the bowl from which a gleam of light is showing. Do not open it. Remember! Do not look inside."

The servant went. He found the house deserted now that the chiefess was no longer there. The beds of shell-trimmed mats lay empty, great calabashes stood open and empty too. High on a shelf a tiny gleam lighted the sleeping house. Wondering, the servant took the bowl, hid it in

his *malo* and made his way back through the crack in the ocean floor.

It was dark when he reached the surface of the sea. Where was the canoe that should be waiting for him? He called but heard no answer. What was in this bowl? What made that gleam of light? Could he not use this thing to signal for the boat? He loosened the tight-fitting cover to peep inside.

The cover came off in his hand. For a moment he saw the treasure, a small gleaming crescent. Then up it sprang, far up, swelling in size and lighting the dark sky! The crescent of the two-day moon shone over sea and land.

Still it shines, sometimes a silvery crescent and sometimes full and bright—making this world lovelier with its light. It is the treasure from the Land Beneath the Sea.

From Hawaiian Antiquities and Folklore *by Fornander.*

The Winning of Mākolea

"**O** Kepaka, I have found for you the most beautiful woman in Hawai'i."

"Tell me about her, uncle," the young man said eagerly. "Is she a chiefess? For I am the son of a chief."

"She is Mākolea, a young chiefess of Kona. Her beauty is as perfect as the beauty of the full moon. Let us go at once to win her, Kepaka, for others will want this lovely girl."

Two days later the young man and his uncle reached the Kona coast to find a crowd gathered on the beach. Canoes were paddling about and men were running. Shouts and wailing filled the air.

"What is it?" the uncle asked. "What has happened?"

"Mākolea is gone," someone replied. "She was surfing with her companions. Many were swimming and surfing. A little while ago a serving woman called for the young chiefess and she could not be found. We fear the waves have carried her out to sea."

"That is not so!" an old man interrupted. "I tell you I saw a canoe at the outer edge of the reef. The young chiefess was lifted in and the canoe paddled away."

For two days Kepaka had thought of nothing but Mākolea—"lovely as the full moon"—and now he did not mean to lose her! "Which way did the canoe go?" he asked and the old man pointed.

Kepaka went to the chief, her father. "I am Kepaka," he said and told the names of his parents. "I have come here to win your daughter as my wife. Give me a canoe that I may search for her."

The old chief looked at the strong young man with broad shoulders and honest eyes. Perhaps he could indeed save the young chiefess. "I will give you a canoe," the father said.

For days Kepaka paddled about asking questions. He heard different stories but at last felt sure that Mākolea had been carried off in a canoe belonging to the high chief of Kauaʻi. This chief must have heard of her beauty and sent man to steal her away. "For he is an evil one!" the young man was told. "The old chief would never give his daughter to such an evil man."

"I shall go and demand that she be returned to her father!" exclaimed Kepaka.

"You cannot! That chief of Kauaʻi is as strong as he is evil. At spear throwing, at wrestling and at boxing no one can beat him. He will kill you! Even if you had strength and skill to escape him at these sports, you would still have to guess his riddles. That is something no one has ever done. Do not go to Kauaʻi, Kepaka."

But the young man answered firmly, "I go to rescue Mākolea and I shall bring her back or I shall die." He started for Kauaʻi.

When Kepaka reached Kauaʻi he was taken before a district chief to whom he told his name and the names of his parents. "You are welcome to Kauaʻi," said the district chief. "Why have you come?"

"I have heard much of your chief," the young man answered. "I have heard of his strength and skill in games. I come to see these sports and perhaps to play against the high chief."

The district chief looked Kepaka up and down. "You are strong and well built," he told him, "but you do not know our high chief. He is a huge man and his skill is equal to his size. Once you have looked upon him you will no longer wish to play against him, but you can see the games. Do you hear shouting? Even now our chief is holding contests. Let us go down and watch."

They found a crowd of men in an open place not far from the chief's house. They pushed their way into the circle and Kepaka saw the high chief. He was a big muscular man wearing a red *malo,* holding a spear of hard wood and strutting about like a fighting cock.

"Ē, little stranger!" he shouted when he saw Kepaka. "Have you come to play with me? Can you throw a spear?"

"I know a little of the sport," Kepaka answered as he stepped into the circle.

"Good!" the high chief shouted. "Good, little one! Shall you or I throw first?"

"You," said the young man bravely. "The stranger should not have first throw."

The crowd drew back to give them room and the high chief and Kepaka faced each other, some distance apart. The chief balanced his spear and hurled it with all his might. Kepaka made a quick movement with his right arm. The chief thought it had gone through Kepaka's body and chanted boastfully:

> "I have hit him!
> My spear never misses when thrown
> At a blade of grass,
> At an ant,
> At a flea,
> This stranger could not escape!"

Kepaka lifted his right arm and let the spear fall to the ground. The high chief stared. Then he chanted:

> "Why did my spear miss its mark?
> You have escaped my first
> But my second will reach you,

O stranger!
This time you cannot escape."

Aiming a bit to the left, he hurled his second spear. Kepaka moved his left arm and caught this also. He held it for a moment then dropped it clattering to the ground.

The chief stared at him while the crowd seemed to hold its breath. At last the chief spoke. "The stranger is a skilled one," he said. "Will you play another game?"

"What reward if I win?" asked Kepaka.

"If you win three games I will give you any reward you ask," the high chief answered, "but if you lose—death!"

Kepaka bowed his head. "If they are games I know, I will play," he promised.

"Wrestling next," said the chief. "Will you wrestle, stranger?"

"I am no wrestler," Kepaka told him. "Is there not some other sport?"

Again the high chief was strutting like a boastful cock. "How about boxing?" he asked. "Does the little stranger know how to box?"

"I have boxed a little," Kepaka answered. "I will try."

The two men moved back and forth inside the circle, each watching for a chance to strike. Out darted the chief's fist. Kepaka was hit and staggered back but did not fall. The chief strutted, sure of victory. Then, before he was on guard, Kepaka struck. His fist caught the chief squarely and the big man fell to the ground with a thud and lay stunned. Again the crowd held its breath.

Slowly the chief recovered and got to his feet. "The stranger is indeed skillful," he said. His voice was faint. "Next comes the riddling. We shall see what the stranger does in that." With those words he turned, leaned on the shoulder of a servant and walked toward his sleeping house.

"Where is the riddling contest?" Kepaka asked his friend.

"It will be here," the district chief replied, "but not today. Our chief wants no more games today. He will send his crier to announce the riddling."

The next day the crier came. The district chief was away but Kepaka heard the crier's shout:

> "Four days from now
> The high chief holds a riddling match.
> Let all men come—
> All who have legs to bring them.
> Let all men come—
> Strangers and native sons."

Kepaka had come out to listen. Now he turned to a servant. "That poor man!" he said, pointing to the crier. "Let us give him food."

"Oh, he eats the scraps from the high chief's table!" said the servant carelessly. "No one ever bothers about him! Besides, he is too dirty."

"That isn't the way we treat men on my island of Hawai'i!" Kepaka said. "Come here, fellow!"

The crier came. "Give him water to wash himself," Kepaka commanded the servants. "Give him a fresh *malo* and shoulder cape. Then set food before him, good food."

Because Kepaka was a chief the servants obeyed. The crier bathed and put on clean garments. Then he sat in the eating house enjoying pork, bananas and *poi*.

When he came out of the eating house, he found Kepaka. He fell on his face before the young man. "O Heavenly One," he said, "as I have gone about Kaua'i no one has ever shown me kindness such as this. How can I serve you? I want to show my thankfulness. I know!" he added, "I can tell the answers to the high chief's riddles. Listen! The first riddle is this:

> Step all around,
> Step to the bottom,
> Leaving an open place;

and the answer is 'house,' for a house is thatched all around from top to bottom, only a doorway is left.

> "This is the second:
> The men that stand,
> The men that stand down,
> The men that are folded.

The answer to that also is 'house.' The upright poles stand, the crossbeams lie down and the thatch is folded."

"I thank you, O Crier," Kepaka said earnestly. "You have more than repaid my kindness."

Four days later the crowd gathered again at the home of the high chief. There was little talk and laughter. The men of Kaua'i did not like these riddling contests. No one could guess the chief's riddles and someone was sure to suffer. This time it would be a stranger.

The high chief strutted out. He saw Kepaka at once. "Ah, there you are, little stranger!" he shouted. "Are you good at riddles?"

"I do not know much about them," Kepaka answered, "but I shall try."

The high chief strutted back and forth as he chanted:

> "Step all around,
> Step to the bottom,
> Leaving an open place."

Suddenly he turned fiercely on the crowd. "Now who can guess that?" he shouted. The crowd was very still, frightened.

After a long moment Kepaka took a step forward. "O Heavenly one," he said, "the answer is 'house,' for a house is thatched all around from top to bottom, only a doorway is left." Kepaka quietly stepped back beside the other men.

The crowd drew a breath of relief but the chief glared at Kepaka. "The little stranger thinks he is clever!" he shouted. "He will not find the next so easy." He looked straight at Kepaka as he chanted the second riddle and his voice was harsh.

> "The men that stand,
> The men that lie down,
> The men that are folded."

For a long moment the chief glared at Kepaka while no one moved. Then again Kepaka took one step forward. "This answer also is 'house,'" he said. "The upright poles stand, the crossbeams lie down and the thatch is folded."

The high chief glared. No one moved or spoke. At last the young man said boldly, "I have won three games, O Heavenly One, and claim my reward."

"What reward do you ask?" The chief's voice sounded small and far away.

"Let the Heavenly One give Mākolea to me."

"So! The stranger has come from Hawai'i for Mākolea." The chief tried to sound boastful and fierce. "Let the young chiefess be brought."

Mākolea was led forth. Kepaka saw that her beauty was indeed as the beauty of the full moon. As for the girl, she went gladly with the man who had come to rescue her.

The two paddled back to Hawai'i. There was rejoicing in Kona over the return of the young chiefess and many days of games and feasting celebrated her marriage to Kepaka.

From Hawaiian Antiquities and Folklore *by Fornander.*

ʻIeʻie and Lehua

Pōkahi and her husband lived at the end of the forest above Waipiʻo Valley. Their home was lonely, for they had no child. They made offering and asked the gods to give them a son or daughter.

The gods heard their prayers and as she slept Pōkahi saw a lovely woman standing by her mats. "You shall have the child you long for," the woman said. "Go down to the Waipiʻo River. There you will see the little one wrapped in soft moss but do not touch her. For thirty days the gods will care for her, then you may take Leaf-of-the-ʻIeʻie-Vine to your home to become your foster child."

Next morning Pōkahi told her husband of this dream and the two went into the valley. As they neared the river they heard, very faintly, a baby's cry. Then a strange thing came to pass. Out of the river grew a tree. It rose before their eyes until it stood full grown. Among its leaves red blossoms gleamed and over these hovered bright-winged birds sucking the nectar.

Long the man and woman gazed at the strange tree whose like they had never seen. Then it sank back into the river, but red mist glowed on the bank beside the place where the tree had stood. From the mist came once more the faint cry of a child. Going closer Pōkahi and her husband saw a tiny baby wrapped in fragrant moss. The woman longed to take it in her arms but remembered the words spoken in her dream, "Do not touch her. For thirty days the gods will care for her."

And so it was. Each day Pōkahi visited the river. She saw the child plump and happy, cared for by her guardian, the red-flowering *lehua* tree. Each day she heard the baby's voice.

When thirty days had passed the strange tree rose once more and its leaves fell, forming a green mat. The tree disappeared but mist above the mat of leaves glowed red and there Pōkahi saw her foster child. Joyfully she took the baby in her arms. The couple carried the little one to their home. They called her Leaf-of-the-'Ie'ie-Vine, the name the gods had given. They gave her loving care and their hearts were filled with joy.

'Ie'ie was a happy child. She lived in the forest and her playmates were the forest winds, the flowers, ferns and shells. When the snails sang at dawn 'Ie'ie sang with them. She made *kī*-leaf whistles and played softly for her friends. So she grew to womanhood.

One night in a dream she saw a young chief, Kawelona. Next morning the young woman told her dream. "Who will find my chief for me?" she asked her friends.

Each answered, "I will go! Send me, O 'Ie'ie."

She chose the chief of the winds to go. At once he started. All about Hawai'i he blew but could not find the dream chief. He journeyed to other islands until, flying toward Ni'ihau, he saw a great flock of little birds. He blew gently among the birds. There were hundreds of them and on their wings they carried a young chief. This was Kawelona.

Now this young chief had seen 'Ie'ie in a dream. Again and again he had seen her but even in dream he did not touch her or hear her voice. Troubled, he went to a wise *kahuna*. "Who is this woman whom I see?" he asked. "She comes in my dream but never speaks to me. Who is she and where shall I look for her?"

The *kahuna* filled a calabash with water and dropped in two flowers. Then he prayed:

"O Sun,
Great ruler of the heavens,

Look down into this bowl of water
And show us there the woman whom we seek."

He looked into the bowl. "I see her," he said slowly. "I see this lovely woman. No one is fairer. She is not a woman of Kaua‘i. Her home is in the shining east. I see her in the forest of Waipi‘o with ferns and flowers about her."

"I shall go to Waipi‘o and find the maiden of my dream," said Kawelona.

Then the wind chief came. "I have come for you, O Kawelona," he began. "I have come to take you to ‘Ie‘ie, your dream maiden."

"I am ready," Kawelona answered eagerly.

In a long white cloud boat they journeyed to Waipi‘o. There Kawelona was made welcome with feasting and with *hula*. There the two young people were married and lived in peace.

The tree which had sheltered Leaf-of-the-‘Ie‘ie-Vine went to the mountain forests. There the *lehua* lives today while bright-winged birds hover above it sucking its nectar. There too lives the *‘ie‘ie* vine, twining loving arms about her guardian.

From Legends of Gods and Ghosts *by Westervelt.*

The Chiefs Who Went
Around Hawai'i

Two young brothers, chiefs of Puna, had long planned to see their island of Hawai'i. "Now is the time," said one. "Puna is peaceful, its gardens flourish and our overseers are men whom we can trust. Let us go now."

They started, these two alone, and climbed the slope of Kīlauea. "This is the very trail which Kalapana climbed," one said, and they thought of the frail old man toiling up until turned back by rain. Their active legs carried them more quickly till they stood beside the fire pit.

Lava seethed and bubbled below but they saw no old woman stirring the fire. Nor did they see the brother of Pele surfing on lava waves or her sisters stringing *lei* or dancing among the flames.

After a night's rest they started on the trail that led along the slopes of Mauna Loa. They crossed rough lava flows. On some, ferns and *lehua* trees were already taking root but much was desolate and lonely.

At last they reached the beach. Here were scattered villages and here they found warm welcome, for word had come already of the chiefs who traveled. The *imu* was filled with food and the two were urged to stay long for rest and entertainment. Wrestling, boxing, *maika* rolling and *hōlua* sledding! Young chiefs came from nearby districts to show their skill.

The two came in sight of Mauna Kea wearing now its helmet of white. They tried to picture the ocean rolling over their great island while the Waipi'o fisherman and his wife cowered together on Mauna Kea's top.

They talked of Pīkoi who also had journeyed here, paddling swiftly with his young men, impatient to reach Waipi'o yet stopping to kill rats, birds or lizards. They drank from the spring his arrow had found and chuckled to think of the surprise and joy of the villagers. In Kohala they saw the bay where Punia had tricked the sharks.

At last they reached Waipi'o, that lovely valley where Kiha had labored as a servant. Waipi'o was full of memories. There Hi'iaka had battled with the whirlwind. There Puapua had raced with the stolen *pū* whose sound had echoed from its walls. There Līloa had ruled, 'Umi had gathered his warriors and the lovely daughter of Keawenui had welcomed Pīkoi on his return.

They walked through the forest of Pana'ewa, beautiful with vines, flowers, ferns and flitting birds. It was hard to picture the fierce battle that had raged when the goddess fought the *mo'o* and the forest was a mess of tangled growth and evil beings.

They saw the crater on Hāla'i Hill where Woman-of-Fire had offered herself that her people might have food. "The chiefs give life to the land," the brothers said solemnly. "We too are chiefs."

Paliuli where Lā'ie had once lived in a golden-feathered house—that land, alone, they did not see, for the gods have hidden it.

After two years they returned to Puna and paused to look at the stone figures still standing on its plain, those who laughed at Pele and felt her punishment. As they neared their own village they heard a sudden shout. Someone had seen them. Soon an eager crowd gathered around the two young men. Shouts of welcome filled the air. "You have been gone long, very long," the people said.

"Our journey has been good," the chiefs replied. "We have indeed seen this great and famous island. But coming home is best of all."

"Your coming is best for Puna," said an old *kahuna* solemnly, "for the chiefs give life to the land."

More days of feasting, games and *hula*. Then the old *kahuna* said, "Come, O Heavenly Ones, for there is one thing more." He led them out where stood two coconut trees with ropes tied to them. The chiefs understood. One stepped forward and laid his hand on the trunk of a young coconut. Men pulled the ropes. Slowly the young tree bent, as if the chief himself had pushed it over, until it lay along the ground. There it was made fast. The other chief laid his hand upon the second tree as it also was bent over.

Then came a serving woman. "O Heavenly Ones," she said, "your sister has a little child—a girl—and waits for you to name her."

"Let her be called Chiefs-that-went-around-the-island," they answered, and so the child was named.

For many years the reclining coconut trees and the woman, Pō'ai, Chiefs-that-went-around-the-island, reminded people of this journey. Both trees and chiefess are gone now but the story lives on, as do these other legends of Hawai'i.

A story of her ancestors told by Mary Kawena Pūku'i.

Glossary
of Hawaiian Words and Names

In Hawaiian "s" is not used to form the plural of a noun. Such Hawaiian words as *lei, he'e, menehune* and *mo'o* may be either singular or plural.

The *'okina,* also known as the glottal stop or hamzah (`'`), and the *kahakō,* also known as the macron (`¯`), are both necessary for correct pronunciation. The *'okina* indicates that at one time a consonant appeared in that place and has since been dropped. The *kahakō* indicates a stressed vowel pronounced somewhat longer than other vowels.

Pronunciation of unstressed vowels:

a as *a* in *a*bove   *o* as second *o* in bronc*o*

e as *e* in b*e*t   *u* as *u* in p*u*ll

i as *i* in s*i*t

Pronunciation of stressed vowels:

ā as *aa* in baz*aa*r   *ō* as *oh* in *oh*

ē as *ey* in th*ey*   *ū* as *oo* in m*oo*n

ī as *ee* in s*ee*

'ā ('aa'): A shout or exclamation of surprise or admiration.

aku (a'ku): A large fish; a kind of ocean bonito.

aloha (alo'ha): Kind feelings; a greeting; affection.

'Aukai ('A'u ka'i): Seafarer; a Kohala man.

'awa ('a'va): A drink made from the root of the *'awa* shrub. It produces sleepiness.

ē (ey'): A call for attention.

Hākau (Haa' ka'u): Brother of 'Umi.

hala (ha'la): The pandanus tree.

Hāla'i (Haa' la''i): A hill near Hilo.

Halemano (Ha'le ma'no): A young man in love with Kama.

Hānai (Haa' na'i): The name taken by 'Umi after fleeing from Waipi'o.

Hā'upu (Haa' 'u'pu): Fortress-like hill on Moloka'i.

Hawai'i (Hawa'i 'i): An island; name of the group.

Hawai'i-nei (Hawa'i 'i ne'i): This Hawai'i.

he'e (he''e): An octopus, commonly called "squid" in Hawai'i.

heiau (he'i a'u): A large place of worship.

Hi'iaka (Hi''i a'ka): Youngest sister of Pele.

Hiku (Hi'ku): Husband of Kāwelu.

Hilo (Hi'lo): A district, Hawai'i; village (present city) of that district.

Hina (Hi'na): A common woman's name; wife of Kū'ula, the fish god; mother of Māui; mother of Kana; mother of Punia; mother of Nī'au; sister of Kīpapa.

hōlua (hoh' lu'a): A long narrow sled.

Huelani (Hu'e la'ni): A dog in a story of Pele.

hula (hu'la): A dance and chant.

'ie'ie ('i'e 'i'e): A vine whose roots are used for basket making, etc.

imu (i'mu): An oven dug into the ground in which food is cooked by means of hot stones.

'Iwa ('I'va): A cleaver trickster and thief.

Ka'analike (Ka'a'na li'ke): Chiefess of 'Ualaka'a, one of the hidden islands of Kāne.

Kaēwe (Ka' ey'we): A chief of Waipi'o.

Kahawali (Ka'ha wa'li): A *hula* master of Puna who had a *hōlua* race with Pele.

Kahiki (Kahi'ki): Tahiti; "Far Kahiki" was a term for any land beyond the place "where the sky rests upon the sea" around the Hawaiian Islands.

kahuna (ka' hu'na): One wise in some kind of work.

Kaialea (Ka'i ale'a): Brother of Kila and son of Mō'īkeha.

Kai'ale'ale (Ka'i 'a'le 'a'le): A chief of man-eating sharks.

Kainoa (Ka' ino'a): A *he'e* fisherman, owner of a lucky cowry shell.

Kalapana (Ka'la pa'na): A village, Puna district, Hawai'i; the man for whom this village is named.

Kalei (Ka' le'i): Mother of Nanaue.

kalo (ka'lo): A vegetable from which *poi* is made; the Tahitian form, *taro,* is in common English use.

Kama (Ka'ma): A girl of Puna loved by Halemano.

kamani (kama'ni): A tree producing oil and flowers prized for their sweet scent.

Kamapua'a (Ka'ma pua''a): A demigod who could take the form of a pig.

Kana (Ka'na): A young chief of Hilo who had the power of stretching to great height.

Kāne (Kaa'ne): One of the great gods.

Kānekoa (Kaa'ne ko'a): A brave man; a man befriended by the god of love.

kapa (ka'pa): bark cloth; the Tahitian form, *tapa,* is in common English use.

kapu (ka'pu): sacred, forbidden; the Tahitian form, *tabu,* is in common English use.

Kaua'i (Kaua''i): An island.

Ka'uiki (Ka''u i'ki): A hill at Hāna, Maui.

Kawelona (Ka'we lo'na): The young chief who married 'Ie'ie.

Kāwelu (Kaa' we'lu): Rippling grass; the wife of Hiku.

Keawenui (Kea've nu'i): Keawe-the-great; he was Keawe-nui-a-'Umi, Keawe-the-great-son-of 'Umi, high chief of Hawai'i.

Kekela (Keke'la): A chiefess of Kona, mother of Queen Emma.

Kepaka (Ke' pa'ka): A young hero of Hawai'i who rescued Mākolea.

kī (kee'): a shrub whose long leaves are used in wrapping food; the Tahitian form, *tī,* is in common English use.

Kiha (Ki'ha): A chief of Waipi'o; son of Pi'ilani, high
    chief of Maui.
Kihapū (Ki'ha poo'): A conch-shell trumpet first belong-
    ing the *menehune,* later to Kiha, chief of Waipi'o.
kīhei (kee' he'i): A shoulder cape.
Kila (Ki'la): Son of Mō'īkeha, high chief of Kaua'i; later
    chief of Waipi'o.
Kīlauea (Kee' la'u e'a): A volcano, Hawai'i.
Kīpapa (Kee' pa'pa): A young chief of the Land Beneath
    the Sea.
koa (ko'a): A tree.
Kohala (Koha'la): A district, Hawai'i.
Kona (Ko'na): A district, Hawai'i.
kōnane (koh' na'ne): A game played with pebbles on a
    gameboard of stone or wood.
Konikonia (Ko'ni koni'a): A chief, a friend of Kīpapa.
Kū (Koo'): One of the great gods.
Kūkali (Koo' ka'li): A man of Kalapana, owner of the
    sacred banana skin.
kukui (kuku'i): The candlenut tree whose nuts are used
    for oil.
Kū'ula (Koo' 'u'la): The fish god.
Lāhainā (Laa' ha'i naa'): A village, Maui.
Lā'ie (Laa' 'i'e): Lā'ieikawai, Lā'ie-of-the-water, chiefess
    of Paliuli.
lauhala (la'u ha'la): Leaf of the *hala* tree; mats plaited of
    these leaves.
lehua (le'hua): A tree; red or white flowers of this tree.
lei (le'i): A necklace; vine or flower wreath for head
    or neck.
Lena (Le'na): name taken by Kila.
Līloa (Lee' lo'a): A high chief of Hawai'i and the father
    of 'Umi.
maika (ma'ika): A game; the rolling stone used in
    this game.

maile (ma'ile): A twining shrub whose fragrance and beauty make it valuable for *lei* and other decorations; a vine.

Ma'inele (Ma''i ne'le): Rat shooter of O'ahu; later a chief.

Maka (Ma'ka): Grandmother of Nohea.

Mākolea (Maa' kole'a): A young chiefess of Kona.

malo (ma'lo): A man's loincloth.

Mānoa (Maa' no'a): A valley, O'ahu.

Maui (Ma'ui): An island.

ma uka (ma' u'ka): Toward the mountains.

Mauna Kea (Ma'una Ke'a): White Mountain (because it is often snowcapped in winter); a volcano, Hawai'i.

Mauna Loa (Ma'una Lo'a): Long Mountain; a volcano, Hawai'i.

menehune (me'ne hu'ne): Small people living in the mountains and forests.

Milu (Mi'lu): Ruler in the land of the dead.

Moloka'i (Mo'lo ka''i): An island.

mo'o (mo''o): A lizard; a giant lizard.

Nanaue (Nana'ue): A son of the shark chief.

Nī'au (Nii' 'a'u): A son of a chief of Far Kahiki.

Nīheu (Nee' he'u): A young chief of Hilo, brother of Kana.

Ni'ihau (Ni''ihau): An island.

Nohea (Nohe'a): Lovely; young chiefess of Kohala.

noni (no'ni): Small tree whose bark and root are used for red dye.

O'ahu (O'a'hu): An island.

'ō'ō ('oh' 'oh'): A bird, some of whose feathers were used for feather capes.

pa'i'ai (pa''i 'a'i): The initial form of pounded *kalo*—it is drier than *poi* and can, therefore, be kept longer.

Paliuli (Pa'li u'li): A legendary land which "the gods have since hidden"; supposed to have been on the slopes of Kīlauea crater above Hilo.

Pana'ewa (Pa'na 'e'va): The giant *mo'o* who ruled
　　the forest above Hilo; now the name of that
　　land section.

pā'ū (paa' 'oo'): A woman's skirt.

Pele (Pe'le): Goddess of the volcano.

Pi'ikea (Pi''i ke'a): A young chiefess of Maui who
　　married 'Umi.

Pi'imai (Pi''i ma'i): One of 'Umi's three companions.

Pīkoi (Pee' ko'i): A boy of Kaua'i who became son-in-law
　　of Keawenui.

Pō'ai (Poh' 'a'i): Nāli'i-po'ai-moku, Chiefs-that-went-
　　around-the-island, a woman of Ka'ū.

poi (po'i): A food made from *kalo*.

Pōkahi (Poh' ka'hi): The foster mother of 'Ie'ie.

pū (poo'): A conch-shell trumpet.

Puakō (Pu'a koh'): Wife of Kainoa.

Puapua (Pu'a pu'a): The yellow dog who got the *pū*.

Puna (Pu'na): A district, Hawai'i.

Punia (Pu'nia): A boy of Kohala who tricked and killed
　　the man-eating sharks.

Pūpū (Poo' poo'): The man who stole *kalo* and sweet
　　potatoes for Kohala.

Pu'u Honu (Pu''u Ho'nu): Turtle Hill near Hilo.

'Ualaka'a ('U'ala ka''a): One of the hidden islands
　　of Kāne.

Uli (U'li): A wise woman of the Hilo district.

'Umi ('U'mi): High chief of Hawai'i.

Waiākea (Wa'i aa' ke'a): Broad waters; a man of Hilo.

Waikīkī (Wa'i kee' kee'): Spurting water; land section,
　　O'ahu.

Wailuku (Wa'i lu'ku): A river, Hilo district, Hawai'i.

Waipi'o (Wa'i pi''o): A valley, Waimea district, Hawai'i.